REDEMPTION

(BALAVAN BOOK TWO)

SYLVIA S. LEE

MEGAN H. LEE

Prologue

With the capture of Victor and the defection of Thom, the Six Year War has finally ended and the Legionnaires are no more. Along with the death of Sovereign Carson, Balavan is a much different place. The Desiderios have become the new protector of the realm. While an election is under way to find a new Sovereign who is not tainted by greed, everyone is working to return things to their former glory.

A mere few months after the fall of the Legionnaires, Balavan is starting to see some form of normalcy. Houses are being rebuilt. Schools are filled with children with laughter. And, flowers are starting to bloom beautifully in the gardens. On the surface, everyone seems to be happy, but there is a sense of unease that seems to be lurking underneath.

Chapter 1: Uneasy Peace

After the disbandment of the Legion, three different groups of men emerge. The first group of the former legionnaires left Balavan. No one knows where they are heading. In some cases, they may not even know themselves.

Most of them have never been outside of Balavan. It is their home and their parents' homes, and their grandparents' homes. It's hard to leave, but they have to. They know that their glory days are gone and there is no point hanging on to a dream once they have awakened.

They simply pack their families and belongings before hitting the road, never looking back.

These are the principled men and women who firmly believe that they have been exiled from their homes unjustly. They have a distasteful taste in their mouths, but know when to fold.

They admit their defeat, but swallow their anger rather than lash out at others. No matter how much they want to, they are too honorable to retaliate with petty crimes or unfounded rumors. Instead, they are hoping that their luck will get better as they seek opportunities and new homes elsewhere.

A second group of men tried to get other gainful employment. Those who prove to be honest and eager are able to find various jobs.

One of the most popular occupations in town is in construction. After the destructions of the war, there is plenty of work to be done. With their physical prowess, many of them become natural builders. While it may be hard work, they soon come to like their new way of life.

Instead of feeling down for losing what they had, many of them start to realize that their new ways of life are much less stressful.

Another popular occupation that former legionnaires gravitate towards is teaching. With the skills and knowledge that they have gained on the job in the Legion, they find that many citizens of Balavan are eager to learn from them, not just in the art of war, but anything ranging from geography to politics.

As the citizens become more and more comfortable with them, former legionnaires are able to find jobs in just about any occupation such as in medicine or art and blending in with everyone else. Even though many are still proud of their past, not many civilians can tell unless they ask.

There are even some who have even joined the ranks of their former enemies, the Desiderios. After watching them carefully, Violet has realized that many of the lower ranking legionnaires are honest fighters who actually believed that what they were doing with the Legion was the right thing to do.

Having been blinded by the ideals that Victor has painted, they were under the impression that everything they did was to protect Balavan. They had no idea that rampant corruption occurred nor did they realize that many of their battles were based on lies with the sole intention of robbing their neighbors and killing innocent people.

This is the group that Violet likes the best, because, like Thom, they have decided to come over to her side on their own accord.

There is a third group of legionnaires who are the troubling kind. These men feel that they have been wronged. Therefore, they are not willing to leave town or get a job which they consider to be demeaning to them.

After all, they were the elite members of the realm and can do anything that they pleased. Why would they need to *work* for a living now?

They try to regroup anyway they can. With the capture of Victor, their generalissimo, and the deaths of key members such as Lieutenant Michael Marcel, and Lieutenant Paul Gillnet, the head of intelligence, however, they no longer have a clear leader.

While it makes their task much harder, some of these men try to lick their wounds by taking refuge in the underground. Ironically, many are hiding in the old hideouts of the Desiderios. It's as if the world has literally turned upside down. Even though many of the underground tunnels and passages have been filled in to prevent others from misusing them, there are many that are still in existence.

So far, these new radicals are laying low and avoiding the possibility of being discovered. They do not have the strength to start anything. When they do come out of hiding, they appear to be just another low abiding citizen blending in with the crowd.

But, Violet knows that, in time, they will be. After all, they were the ones who had no problem plundering in the first place. Why would they stop now?

More of a reason for the Desiderios to keep a close eye on them. The problem is the question of how to identify them. Despite the bitter taste in their mouths, this group of former legionnaires is putting on a good show. They have discarded anything that may connect them with the old government and appear to be happy with the new regime.

*

As for Thom, he stands by his own convictions. He knows that ratting out his father is a sacrifice that he had to make, no matter how much it hurts him or those he loves. As his reward, he now inherits everything that his father once owned for his role in taking down the Legion. Even though Trip knows very well that much of it was bought with blood of innocent people, it is up to Thom to decide how he should make retributions for his father's sins. In addition, having been a general with the Legionnaires, Trip and Violet have decided to give him the rank of a Colonel, a respectable position among the Desiderios, one that is not so high that it would make existing officers jealous, but high enough not to be insulting.

While Thom is more than happy with the position that he has been given, he feels an immense amount of remorse for a great many things. The one that sticks out the most in his mind is having turned against his own father, which is the only deed that he is personally guilty of doing. His sense of betrayal is eating him alive. No matter what this man did, he is still his father and no father deserves to be stabbed in the back by his own flesh and blood regardless of how rotten he may be.

There are many nights when Thom can't fall asleep because of his guilt. Even his exquisitely designed bed that was the most comfortable thing that he'd ever slept on could help him go to sleep.

As he learned the hard way, no amount of material goods can let him forget. Instead, he keeps going over different scenarios of how he could have saved his father and Balavan at the same time. Why couldn't he have simply confronted him? Would Victor have backed down if he heard the truth from his own son? Could he have recruited his mother to try to convince him? Would he have listened to her if not him? Or, perhaps, he could have threatened to abandon him if he did not stop his greedy and immoral ways. Of course, none of it matters anymore. The damage is done.

He knows that this decision has torn his family apart. His mother Amelia is absolutely inconsolable. She refused to see him ever since her husband's imprisonment. To publicize her disdain for him, she has disowned him completely. Because Thom has inherited all of his father's possessions, his mother has moved out of their home. Thanks to Victor's generosity to his own wife, he has given her a beautiful vacation home in the outskirt of town. Because she retains her own possessions, she still has a place to call home. She has also taken all of the servants with her, which is fine by Thom.

After all that she and Victor have gone through for Thom, she simply cannot fathom why he did what he did. What makes Amelia's hatred for her son that much worse is that she thinks Victor is dead. With no other living relative, she has no one else to lean on, but herself. There are two main reasons for this deceit.

First, Trip has no intention of letting anyone outside of a handful of trusted members of the Desiderios know that the former Generalissimo is still alive, including his own wife and son.

After all, Victor's reputation, like that of El Diablo's, is bigger than life itself. As far as many people are concerned, he might as well have been 8 feet tall and can crush a boulder with his bare hands. His reputation made him appear to be wise beyond imagination.

Because many former members of the now defunct army have never met him in person, this image of a great warrior still stands in their minds. If his former followers catch wind that he is still alive, they may use his memories to resurrect the Legion. In a world that is so easily influenced by gossips and hearsays, it would be a very easy task. One simple rumor can easily turn him into a martyr or spark another revolution.

Second, as a part of the punishment, Trip makes a point of not letting Victor know anything about the fate of his family members. By letting his wife think that he is deceased, she would not make any attempt to contact him.

In turn, Trip wants his arch enemy to think the worst and let it eat him alive. He wants his imagination to run wild and believe that his loved ones are facing all the tortures and degradations that Victor was capable of when he pillaged his victims' home towns. Although Trip trusts Thom not to reveal this secret, it is just safer to leave him out of it. He knows that if anyone wants to know anything about Victor, they would approach his own son first. Besides, Thom has enough to deal with. He does not need to add yet another weight on his chest.

*

As for Balavan itself, things are also returning back to normal. After losing its former sovereign David Carson, the citizens of the dominion have elected a new one. To ensure that they do not put someone as weak minded as Carson, they want a leader of the Desiderios to hold the dominion's highest political position. Because of Trip's reclusive demeanor, he made sure to let them know he had absolutely no interest in the position.

While the public wants to nominate Violet, she has also graciously declined the offer. She never considered herself to be a politician. In fact, she is not a fan of one, because she has never met one who is not corrupt. Of course, that is not to say that there isn't an honest one, just that she finds that the power of a political position often gets the best of men, even the good ones. If she were to place herself in that

6

position, she would simply feel dirty and be degrading herself.

Instead, the citizens elect Garret, one of her former subordinates. Being the intelligence officer for the Desiderios, he has intimate knowledge of everything that goes on within Balavan. His obsessive compulsive behavior makes him ideal for this role because it makes sure that he is on top of everything. With his eagle eyes and propensity to sniff out crime, the citizens are hoping that the days of leaders sneaking in favors under the table are over.

As for Violet, she sincerely hopes that he can rise above temptation. In order to quell her fears, she paid a visit to Garret during his election campaign.

"So, how are things?" she asks as she scans his campaign headquarter.

"Good. Thank you for paying me a visit, Violet. This is a great honor!" Garret replies with a genuine smile.

"Do you need any help?" Violet asks lightheartedly.

"From you? Definitely!" he says excitedly as he pulls her to a desk. "I would love it if you can give me some advice on a project that I am hoping to work on once I am elected."

Violet is glad that he is not above asking for assistance. He also seems to be genuinely passionate about this job. Everything seems to be in shape. She has never seen him so excited.

He has his entire agenda ready on the walls, including everything from building more education centers to getting rid of corruption. If he keeps these promises, he is definitely the man for the job. Despite her reservations, Garret seems to be going in the right direction immediately after being given the job.

After he's elected he makes sure to clean up the sovereign's mansion. He has removed every potentially corrupt aide and replaced them with people he trusts or well-known experts in their field.

One of these members is Max, who is in charge of engineering efforts. Returning to his old self, Max is back in his parents' estate. Even though he suspected that his parents are not coming back. This is the first time that he has returned home knowing that as a *fact*.

The house now feels emptier than ever before. Nevertheless, he is determined to continue his father's work in the laboratory and keep his parents memories fresh.

Additionally, he also knows that he is not alone in this world. Having found his aunt and uncle is definitely a positive part of his experience during the war. Now, he has someone new to count on. Even though the rebel headquarters is still standing exactly where it has always been, there is no longer a need to guard it. Max's Aunt Lillian and Uncle Adam have decided to leave the reclusive mountain and return to the way of life that they have known and loved for so long. They have disarmed all of the booby traps in the gates and covered any remnants of them.

After having left the tribe for such a long time, they are eager to return to their extended families. They cannot wait to introduce their son Sean to them and teach him all about the Kerbasy way of life. Of course, a part of them is worried that he may not like it as much as they hope since he has been a city dweller his entire life. But, that is more of a reason to leave now before he gets any older.

*

As for other members of the Desiderio, their lives have also changed. Now that Balavan is back to its peaceful days, Trip decided to take a hiatus from all of this fighting. While Violet misses Trip, she also has more important things in her mind – an escaped leader of the former Legions.

Although the Desiderios have captured almost all of master minds, there is one who has eluded them – Major Brandon Fouke. Unlike the others who are loyal to the Legion, this slippery servant is all for himself. There is no telling what he really has planned.

All she knows for certain is that he is dangerous. From what she knows of him, he is all about getting the most out of everything – for himself. He has no moral or conscience. If destroying an entire village does not contradict with his personal gains, he will not even bat an eye before annihilating every man, woman, and child. At the same time, he is very shrewd. He knows when to make himself scarce. That explains why he was able to escape when everyone else was captured.

The question is where? The fact that he is an ordinary looking man makes it easy for him to blend in without needing a much of a disguise of any kind. Being medium build and height with brown hair and blue eyes, he can be anybody and anywhere.

To make it more difficult to locate him, Fouke was an expert at disguise. He knew how to make it especially hard for them to find him. He knew the ins and outs of deceiving people.

In addition, he is a very good and convincing liar, when he wants to, that is. Because he is very self-confident, very few people ever question him. He was able to get away with just about everything.

Ever since the end of the war, Violet sent out scouts in every possible location where he would be, but none of them has not come up with any good lead. Despite some possible sightings, no one knows for sure if it is him or not. She knows that this is one fugitive that must be captured or this peace may be short-lived.

Chapter 2: Trozos Island

While Violet is searching high and low for him, Fouke is getting comfortable in his new hiding place. He has been here for nearly a month and is ready to venture out and mingle with the public.

Unfortunately, it's not as easy as it sounds. In order to elude the Desiderios, Fouke had to go where they wouldn't look for him, Trozos Island, a piece of rock that is filled with aborigines who practice cannibalism, or at least the Balavans think it is.

Right after the Legionnaires lost the war, Fouke ran to his hideout for exactly this purpose and made sure to get rid of everything that could connect him to his former life. He was careful in making sure to destroy everything, shredding them into oblivion.

Because of his outward arrogance, even those closest to him cannot imagine that he would give up all of his worldly goods in order to disappear. Yet, the truth of the matter is he has never let anyone in the world know the *real* him. What they don't realize is the extent he will go to in order to survive is vast. Contrary to his public persona, he will never let something like an ego get in his way.

In addition, he is more resourceful than most people give him credit for. Because he seems to be too lazy to do anything that is not a part of his assigned duties, no one really realized that he is actually good at a lot of things. For instance, he is quite an accomplished craftsman. During his time as a hunted criminal, he created a raft complete with sail and paddles out of fallen tree branches in the dark in relative silence. Although it took him almost three weeks to finish it, the final product could make the greatest of master carpenters proud.

To be sure that he is not being followed, he deliberately set sail from the opposite direction as his intended destination in order to throw off anyone's scent. Then, he takes the long route to Trozos Island. Packing light, he has nothing but several canteens full of water and a fishing rod. After weeks of grueling voyage and rough sea, he has never been so glad to see palm trees.

The thought of possibly being eating alive upon landing didn't enter his mind until he got onto the beach, exhausted. Then, he hears rustling in the bushes. As he gets up slowly, he knows the last thing he wants to do is to provoke them. There is no telling how many of them there are. During a time like this, there is no way he can win by sheer force. Besides, he has never been a great fighter. Instead, he relies on his brains to survive in this world, which is a definite must in this situation.

Raising both of his arms, he says in a firm but calm voice, "I come in peace."

The rustling sound continues, but no one comes out. Without being able to see who he is dealing with, it's difficult to determine what his next approach is. Nevertheless, he wants to be prepared just in case. Then, he slowly moves closer to his raft. This serves two purposes. First, if arrows or other weapons start to shoot out from the trees, he can use the raft as a cover. Second, if they plan on eating him, he wants to show them that there are other sources of food available. Even though he has no idea what they want to eat, he has to chance it. On his raft are a dozen fish that he has caught for himself, but this seems to be a better use for them.

"OK," Fouke thinks to himself, "the ball is in their court now."

After standing there motionless for a few more minutes, he is beginning to wonder if it is indeed people behind those trees. With his hands still up, he announces, "I mean

12

you no harm. I am going to put my hands down now. They are starting to get tired."

He knows if these people are actually cannibals, they can care less whether or not his is getting tired. On the other hand, if these are civilized people, he is hoping that they find his lighthearted comment as a friendly gesture. After staying put for another twenty minutes, he figures the danger is over. Whatever it was in the trees must have left.

Armed with hidden dagger, he walks towards the area where he heard the sound to check it out. All the while, he makes sure that his hands are open in case that he is still being watched. When he reaches the spot, he takes a sigh of relieve. There are no sign of another human being there anymore, but there were. Although he is not a scout, he can tell that there are faint prints in the ground.

As he looks closer, a smile comes to his lips. These are made by shoes, not feet. In fact, they are not just any shoes. Based on the imprints, they look like heavy duty combat boots. Aren't the aborigines supposed to be backward people who eat intruders? If so, they wouldn't be wearing shoes, at least not this type, would they? He is hoping that the tale of cannibalism is fabricated, or at least highly exaggerated. Perhaps, someone spread it to deter others from coming. If that is true, they have done a marvelous job. No outsider has set foot on this island for decades.

Then again, if they did, who are they? What are they hiding? And, most importantly, how far will they go to keep their lie? It may seem strange, but now Fouke's smile fades and he is genuinely concerned. Maybe it's because the prospect of being eaten is too foreign of a concept, but he is not as worried about it as being ambushed by trained soldiers. Perhaps, it's because the latter option is all too familiar to him and much more likely. Or possibly, it's because no one from Balavan who has set sail for this island has ever returned.

Regardless of the reason, Fouke is on high alert. Even if they are not cannibals, they certainly do not welcome visitors. As far as he is concerned, they are as bloodthirsty as one. He must find out more about the natives of this island before it's too late.

Before long, he sees animal traps hiding in the tall grass. Even though they don't look very sophisticated, they have metal parts, which signal that the inhabitants know something about blacksmithing and have tools. By itself, this doesn't prove anything because many types of people hunt animals regardless of the level of their civility. As he gets closer to examine the contraption, however, someone hits him in the back of his head.

*

Slowly, Fouke opens his eyes. He is chained to a post in a simple hut. He is struggling to free himself when a man comes in and says something to him in a foreign language.

"I am sorry. I don't know what you are saying."

The man repeats his previous command louder as if he can understand it better. Shaking his head, he says, "I don't understand."

Frustrated, the man unlinks the chains from the post and drags him outside.

Once he steps out, the sun is beaming in his eyes and he cannot make out what he is looking at. Then, panic sets in. He sees a bonfire with a roasting rack. A group of natives are sitting around it.

"Are they going to cook me?!" Fouke asks himself.

Terrified, he tries to run, but the chains stops him within five feet.

The man takes out a large sword and says something else.

"Please don't eat me," he begs. "I don't have much meat in me. And, I am all dirty and dried up after my voyage. If you want food, I will be glad to go hunting for you."

Although the natives do not understand what he is saying, they are all laughing.

Puzzled, he asks, "What's so funny?"

The man who dragged him out of the hut just keep laughing at him and saying something he doesn't understand. Then, Fouke is not sure how to feel? Is he off the hook? Is this just a big practical joke they play on people who come onto the island? Or, are they still going to eat him but think he looks ridiculous? One thing is for sure – he is utterly confused.

Then, the crowd quiets down and parts way, creating a path towards the largest hut in the middle of the village. Sitting in a large wicker seat in the front is an old man with a crown of flowers and a scepter made of ivy and twine. Next to him is a young woman who is also adorned with a beautiful crown and jewelry made out of blossoms. On both sides of them are two large and menacing looking guards armed with many, many dangerous weapons.

The old man starts to speak. For a second, Fouke panics. He knows this is the chief of the tribe. If he doesn't like what he says, he can have him killed on the spot. The problem is he is speaking the same foreign language as the other people. What is he going to do? As he starts to sweat, he hears an angelic voice coming to the rescue. The young girl next to him is translating.

"What are you doing in our village?" She asks.

Trying to calm down, he musters his most professional and diplomatic poise and says, "I apologize, your majesty, for intruding."

As he speaks, the young woman is translating.

Not wanting to let anyone find out that he is a war criminal, Fouke continues and says, "I got lost on my voyage and have been marooned on your island."

Judging from the chief's serious expression, Fouke can tell that he does not believe him, causing his heart to pound faster and faster with each passing second. Ordinarily, he is an excellent liar. He can spin anything out of thin air and sound convincing, but today, he just cannot think of a good story to tell. Then, again, he has never faced hundreds of natives surrounding him at once before, especially after being very hungry and thirsty from his journey.

The young woman then resumes her translation and asks, "Where were you headed?"

"Nowhere, I was on a leisure fishing trip and was caught in a storm."

As soon as the words left his mouth, Fouke can almost kick himself. He knows the chief can tell it's a lie. Even though these are natives, they certainly know their own weather patterns. Since there were mostly clear skies in the sea, it was probably relatively sunny, here, too.

His fear is confirmed immediately when the chief becomes angry and shouts out some commands. Immediately, the guards point their swords at him. Then, the young woman says, "We do not believe you. We will give you one more chance to tell us the truth."

"OK, OK! I am from Balavan. I escaped there because of the war," Fouke says.

Because this is partially true, the chief is not sure whether or not to believe him, but seems to want to give him the benefit of the doubt.

The chief and the young woman continue the interrogation with a serious face and ask, "What is your name?

Since Fouke cannot risk being discovered here or anywhere, he obviously lies and says, "My name is Gavin Anderson."

He does not know why he picks that name, but it sounds good enough to him. Gavin Anderson is common enough of a name that also sounds real. Besides, once that name leaves his lips, he has to remember and stick with it.

She then asks, "Why have you chosen to escape here? Haven't you heard? We eat people like you."

Upon hearing those words, a chill goes down Fouke's back, but he manages to keep it together.

Taking a chance, he says, "Yes, I have heard the rumors, but I do not believe that you do."

Turning angry, the chief shouts as the young woman tries to keep her composure and says, "Are you calling us liars?"

Trying to defuse the tension, he says, "Absolutely not! When I saw how beautiful the island is, I knew the rumors cannot be true. When I landed, I didn't see any signs of barbarism."

"If it's barbarism you want, it's barbarism you will get."

The chief has heard enough. Its one thing to see him squirm in his boots, but it's another to hear sycophancy. No longer amused, he shouts commands, which requires no translation. The guards wrestle to the ground and put him in chains.

Fouke continues to protest. "No, your majesty. Please, I come in peace. I have no intention of insulting you! Please hear me out. I can help you!"

"We don't need your help," the young woman translates as he is being dragged out as he continues to shout his protests.

*

The truth of the matter is, the Chief Cai *is* curious as to why this stranger has landed on his hometown. More importantly, he wants to know if he is a spy who is endangering his home or a person he can use. Despite having a reputation for being barbaric, the chief is very wise, following the footsteps of his father who started the rumor about cannibalism on his island. Before he started it, his people constantly had to fight off intruders who threatened their homes.

The Trozians are peace and fun loving people who are also very trusting, so much so that their doors have no locks. Anyone who enters their door is simply welcomed. In fact, they had no problem with leaving their possessions out in the open any time of the day, knowing that no Trozian will ever steal it.

Unfortunately, outsiders soon heard that they were easy targets and began coming ashore to take advantage of their hospitality. Crimes ranging from petty theft to murder spiked about 50 years ago. Chief Cai's father knew that he had to do something before his home is destroyed. At that time, he sent out undercover intelligent officers to surrounding areas to start the rumor. To make the story stick, they even told horrifying tales of near escapes from being eaten alive.

Meanwhile, the old chief sentenced all outsiders who committed a crime against them to life in prison, never to return to their home countries. To make it even more realistic and terrifying to outsiders who have not gotten off of their boats, he put the heads of deceased criminals all around the beaches along with piles of bones. Even though they are animal bones, it's difficult for anyone to tell the difference from a distance. There are also crudely made signs that have worn off red letters on them simulating blood to ward off intruders.

One of the men he sent overseas is his own son, the current chief. As fate would have it, Cai was assigned to Balavan and is very well aware of the people and culture there. To be able to immerse himself there without arousing any suspicion, he is also very fluent in the Balavan language. The usage of a translator is merely a ruse to keep up his reputation as a savage. Although he has not returned to the dominion since coming home, over the years, he has sent scouts there as well as other neighboring lands to make sure that the rumors remain intact and that no foreigner even thinks about invading or do anything to threaten Trozos Island.

After speaking with Fouke, Cai knows that the intruder is just another self-serving man who wants to take advantage of his homeland. The question is why? Besides hiding from the Desiderios, what exactly is he planning on doing there? If he is merely seeking refuge, there is really nothing to worry about. If he is looking for revenge, however, this can spell trouble. The chief has no intention of letting anyone bring the war to him or anywhere near his island.

Although Fouke played a relatively large role in the Legionnaires, he made sure that he was rarely in public view for this very purpose. If he remained in the background, people would not be able to connect his face with his name. So far, it has been proven quite effective. Neither Cai nor any of his men have ever heard of a Gavin Anderson before.

From the way he is dressed, looks, and even smells, he certainly does not have the appearance of a military man. After being in the open sea for so long, his hair is a tangled mess. His beard is unruly and his clothes are torn and wet. His skin is dried and encrusted with mud and filth and his teeth are yellow and dingy. Even those who know him well probably couldn't recognize him without staring into his eyes.

On the other hand, his scouts have told him about a war criminal named Brandon Fouke who has disappeared. Although they do not know what he looks like, they do know his military history and his role in the war. From the report, Cai knows that this escapee has an evil heart and can potentially destroy his people. Hence, Fouke has not exactly pulled the wool over the chief's eyes just quite yet.

After comparing what he has heard about the war criminal against what he has just witnessed, however, Cai has his doubts as to whether or not this is indeed the same man. After all, how can a Major be so *unprofessional*? He seems to be more worried about being eaten alive than anything else. Aren't officers of the Legion supposed to be very proud men? He certainly doesn't behave like one.

Then again, he can just be a very good actor. As a former spy himself, he knows very well how acting can come in very handy when faced with the enemy. During times of imminent danger, pride needs to take a backseat to survival skills. This can very well be what this stranger is doing.

Gathering his advisors into his hut, Cai asks, "So, what do you think? Should we hear him out?"

"I don't see any harm in talking with him," says the first advisor.

As the chief looks around the room, a few others nod their heads in agreement. Like usual, there are always those who have no real opinion and simply go along with whoever is the most vocal. Then, he looks at Nimue, his daughter and the translator, and says, "What do you think?"

"I don't trust him."

"Why not?"

"I can see it in his eyes. Even though he says one thing, his eyes say another."

"Please explain," Cai says as he looks around the room. He is not just trying to get her answer, but trying to teach the rest of the men a thing or two about reading body language.

"I think he has been acting the entire time. He is constantly looking for an exit strategy. When I was talking with him, I can tell that he was studying both of us. He wants to see if we are gullible." Then, the princess laughs and says, "But I think you gave him a run for his money, Poppy. He looked a little scared at times. I think we have convinced him that we are barbaric skeptics."

"That's good," Cai says as he nods. "We want to put the fear in him. Otherwise, he can be a problem. Who wants to be the one to listen to what he has to say?"

"I will," Nimue volunteers.

"OK, but I need another volunteer to go with you."

Nimue looks a little annoyed that her father does not trust her with this mission by herself.

Then, he explains, "If you go, you will be there to play the part of a translator. He must not know that you are anything more than that. Otherwise, he may try to do you harm in order to get to me."

"I am not a little girl, Poppy."

"I know that, but, like you, I don't trust him."

"I will go with the princess," Albin says as he raises his hand like a shy little school boy.

Smiling, Cai nods and says, "Good, that's settled then. Give the man some time to sulk in jail first. You two will go first thing in the morning when he has calmed down a bit."

Chapter 3: Polar Opposites

Cai knows that Albin wants to make a good impression on him and his daughter. The young man has been trying to get Nimue's attention for years, but she has always brushed him off. Being intelligent, handsome, tall, and strong, he can get any woman on the island, but not her.

Even though she has never been mean or rude to anyone, she has never said more than a few words or spent more than a few minutes in the same room with him before taking off. He has never understood why and wants to use this chance to get to know her better.

Albin feels like his entire life has been leading up to this moment. This is his opportunity to prove to her and her father that he is worthy of her hand. Ever since they were children, he has always liked her. Being two years older than her, they practically grew up together. Because his father was a very close advisor to the chief, he has had many chances to visit her in her home. Yet, she has always kept her distance.

Following the advice of his father, he constantly goes above and beyond to impress her. When she started to learn to be a translator, he hit the books very hard to learn different languages. When she took up a musical instrument, he quickly hired a tutor and perfected it. No matter what he did, it was to no avail.

It's not like there is an obvious competition in the mix. In fact, she seems to keep a distance from everyone, men and women. She seems to enjoy spending time at home with her books the most. It does not matter the topic. It can be fiction or non-fiction, action or romance, history or science. Albin has tried reading as much as he can and on any subject that he can, trying to find out what is the allure.

Eventually, he got tired of reading indoors when it is so beautiful outside.

Before long, he became very athletic, attracting the attention of other women on the island. He has gone on many dates with them, hoping *that* will get her attention.

It hasn't. Finally, after turning 21, he has run out of things to try. The only thing left to do is to try to join Chief Cai's council. Although he is a lot younger than the other advisors, the chief agreed because he knew that Albin is intelligent and has heart, two very important attributes. This is the first real mission he has been on and he wants to make sure that it is a success.

Arriving outside of the chief's door, he quietly asks, "Are you ready, Princess Nimue?"

"Yes" is the only response he gets.

Slowly, she emerges from the hut as the sun shines brightly on her face, making her squint.

"Beautiful morning, isn't it?" Albin says trying to start a conversation.

She nods without saying another word. As they walk towards the jail cell, she walks a few steps behind him, which makes him uncomfortable. Why does she not walk next to him? It's not like he has an infectious disease or anything, but sometimes he feels like that is how she sees him. As he turns back to look at her, he figures there is nothing to lose. It's not like he is making any headway with her no matter what he does. So, here goes nothing.

"Why do you not like me?" Albin asks flatly.

Surprised at how direct the question is, Nimue just looks at him blankly and says, "What do you mean?"

"Come on, don't play coy. You know I have liked you since you were five years old. No matter what I do, you always ignore me."

24

"I do not. I am here with you, aren't I?"

"This doesn't count. You are only here because the chief agreed for us to be on the same mission. Even then, you refuse to walk next to me. Am I really that disgusting to you?"

"Wow, you are one sensitive fellow, aren't you?"

"What? After sixteen years of getting the cold shoulder, you think I am being overly sensitive?"

"Yes."

Frustrated and a little embarrassed, he tries to brush off her remark and turn the table back on her. "Well, you still haven't answered the question. Why are you avoiding me?"

"I am not. I just don't like to compete with others."

"Compete? Who do you have to compete with? You have always been my one and only."

"Not according to about a dozen other women in town."

Ah, it's like a weight has lifted off of his shoulders. For the first time in his life, he finally hears her acknowledge his existence.

"If you know about them, then you should also know that they are all just friends."

"Do they know that?"

"Of course, why wouldn't they? I have always been a perfect gentleman with each one of them. I have never tried to lead them on or make any promises that I don't intend on keeping."

"Some women may consider that to be a terrible tease."

"What are you talking about?"

"By taking them out on a date, you have started something with each one of them. Regardless of what you think you have done, they are thinking that there may be a future between you, even if you do not say anything to make them think that there is one, that is, as long as you do not come out and spell it out to them. "

"That is crazy."

"No, it's not."

"Is that how you feel, too?"

"About what?"

"About being on a date – that there may be a future with your date just by agreeing to go out with him."

"Of course not."

"Then, why do you think this way?"

"Because I can hear them talk about you."

Intrigued, Albin asks, "Really? Who?"

"I don't know their names – just another dizzy airhead who is smitten by you."

Shaking his head, Albin tries once more to get back to his original question. "Besides your dislike of competition, which I am not sure if it's true or not, why do you not like me?"

It seems Albin hasn't learned yet. Upon hearing those little words, Nimue rebukes with, "So, now you are calling me a liar?"

"Wow, I don't believe this! How did you just turn this on me – again? Why am I the bad one in this conversation? No, I am not calling you a liar. I am simply saying that you are avoiding the question with non-answers."

"Fine, I don't like you because you try too hard."

Finally, that is something Albin can believe. Yes, he admits. He does try too hard, but that is because he has been trying for so long with nothing to show for. With

26

every failure, he tries harder. After so many years, even he can tell that he is starting to suffocate her with attention.

"I am sorry. I only do it because…" Albin looks into eyes for the dramatic effect before finishing the sentence. "Well, I love you."

Rolling her eyes, Nimue says, "Oh, give me a break. I am sure you say that to every woman you see."

"That's not true. Ask any of them. You are the only one I have said those words to. I am sure you know I am telling the truth."

Yes, she does know that he is telling the truth, but she does not really care. Since she has known him her entire life, she has always considered him a brother more than anything else. All of the efforts that he has made to get her attention just make him sound desperate. While her brains tells her that she should be flattered that he is doing all of this just for her, her heart tells her that he is coming on too strong and doesn't have a chance.

In either case, it just feels weird having this conversation with him. When the jail cell is in view, she takes a sigh of relief. Finally! This conversation can end! Immediately, she returns to her subservient role as a translator and walks behind him again. He, in turn, follows suit. Standing up straight, he walks confidently towards the intruder.

*

"Good morning, Mr. Anderson," Albin starts as Nimue translates.

"Good morning," Fouke replies with a strained voice.

He has not had a very good night. While no jail cell is ever comfortable, this one is certainly anything but. Although the islanders are good enough not to chain him, the accommodation is less than desirable. In addition to a terrible draft and a damp, leaky roof, there are no modern furnishings of any kind. Instead of a bed, it has a pile of straws. Instead of a toilet, it literally has a deep hole with a round wooden cover. The entire cell smells terribly. He can also hear rodents running around. Needless to say, he was unable to sleep well despite the fact that it was the first night he spent on dry land for weeks.

"The Chief has sent me to speak with you. What is it you wanted to tell us?" Albin continues.

Trying to regain his composure, Fouke replies, "Please thank you chief for his kindness. I wanted to offer him my services as a carpenter. As you can see from the sail boat that I arrived in, I am quite skilled at building things."

"Is that it?" Albin asks in a serious tone.

Sensing that the conversation is not going well, Fouke says, "I can do other things, too. I am willing to do anything his majesty wants me to do to prove to him that I am sincere and not a threat to anyone on this island."

"What exactly do you have in mind?"

Well, that is a loaded question if he has ever heard one. Fouke knows that he has to be very careful answering this one. Otherwise, he may end up doing filthy jobs that no one on the island wants to do for the rest of his life. At the same time, he does not want to sound like he is not willing to go beneath him in order to prove himself. It's a very touchy subject. He decides to send out feelers to see how the delegate thinks.

Without getting specific, he replies, "I am willing to work for nothing but room and board."

Not satisfied with the answer, Albin continues, "What else?"

"I can teach your children my trade for free."

"And?"

Fouke is starting to get nervous. Obviously, the chief's delegate wants to hear something specific, but he is not sure what it is. Is this a trick? Maybe if he looks a little pathetic, he will feel sorry for him and give up the line of questioning.

Looking frustrated, Fouke says, "I don't know what else his majesty wants me to do. Please enlighten me."

Albin seems to take the bait. He says, "If that is all you have to say, I will relay the message to his majesty. Good day."

As Albin and Nimue turn away from the jail cell, Fouke says, "Please, wait. Please. Is there any way you can let me out of this cell? I have not done anything wrong."

"That is for his majesty to decide," Albin replies and continues to depart.

Seething under his breath, Fouke cannot believe he is stuck in the cell again. He is starting to wonder if he made the right decision to come here at all. Trying to look at the positive side, he sees two good things that are going for him. First, this island is most definitely not filled with cannibals. Second, he has not seen anyone from Balavan yet, which means his secret is still safe for now.

*

As Albin and Nimue return to the chief's hut, they both walk silently and feet away from one another. "Is it possible that I have made things worse with the princess?" Albin ponders to himself. He really wants to ask if they have a chance at all, but he does not want to hear the answer. He knows if he asks now, he definitely will not get the answer that he wants.

Meanwhile, Nimue is wondering when he is going to start talking again. She knows he will. It's just a matter of when. Even if it's not today, it may be the next day or the next week. Knowing him as well as she does, she knows he will not just drop it and leave her alone. That's probably another reason why she is trying to avoid him.

After they reach the hut, the chief smiles understandingly. He can tell from both of their expressions that they have had an awkward discussion, which most probably ended in rejection. He puts his arm on Albin's shoulder and says, "How did it go?" He purposely leaves the question somewhat vague because he wants to see how this poor young lad is going to answer.

Smiling, Albin says, "It was ok."

"Ah, always the professional, leaving his heart behind," Cai says to himself. Albin is obviously referring to the mission rather than his daughter. So be it.

Albin then recounts his conversation with Anderson with the rest of the council members. As they listen, they each nod their heads like a bunch of clones while Cai has a slightly worried look on his face.

"What's the matter, Poppy?" Nimue asks curiously.

"So, she does know how to read people's feelings," Albin says sarcastically to himself. This confirms it. She has been pretending not to know he feels about her when she can clearly read body language, fairly well and quickly, too. She just chooses to ignore his. Chief Cai smiles again as he looks at Albin's frustrated face.

Then, he says, "I need something more constructive than a bunch of nodding. What do you really think of the stranger's request?"

As he looks around the room, the advisers all look at one another. Then, one of them says, "I think we should give him a chance to prove himself."

"OK. Why?" the Chief replies.

"Because I think we don't have anything to lose."

"Why wouldn't we? Since he has already said that he is a great craftsman, what stops him from making things to use against us? We also have no way of verifying his story. The only thing we know about him is his name and his skills. For all we know, that is a lie, too."

As always, there's a bunch of nodding with whispers.

Then, another adviser quietly says, "We shouldn't trust him."

"Because?" the Chief asks impatiently.

Looking around at his peers nervously, the man says, "Because he is an outsider and we don't know anything about him. It's better to be safe than sorry."

"OK, I hear you."

Again, there are more nodding. Even those who nodded in support of giving Anderson a chance is nodding in the argument against him.

Chief Cai has just about enough. He looks at Albin and asks, "What do you think?"

"I think we should give him a chance."

"What about you, Nimue?"

"I don't."

Even though he is a little frustrated that there is no consensus, Chief Cai has already expected this. When there is no clear answer, these two almost always have very different opinions. Albin is typically the optimist. He wants to believe in the good of people and hoping that one day everyone will do the right thing. This certainly shows in his determination to win over Nimue's heart despite his lack of success.

His daughter, on the other hand, is the near opposite. She is suspicious of others, especially outsiders. She has heard of all of the stories about outsiders taking advantage of their people in the past many times before. Being a princess, she is also used to people being nice to her, not for herself, but for what she can do for them. Hence, she hardly trusts anyone based on blind faith. She always has to study them carefully first before letting anyone in.

Secretly, the Chief has always liked Albin and thinks he is perfect for his daughter. After knowing him his entire life, he has not found a single real fault in the young man. Despite his somewhat dubious reputation as a ladies man, he certainly seems sincere and honest when it comes to his affections toward Nimue.

Nevertheless, publicly, Cai has no opinion towards the relationship. He wants the decision to be hers and hers alone. No one should influence her happiness, not even her own father. If she comes to him for advice, he will most certainly give it to her, but not a second before then. It's sad that her mother is not here for her. She died during childbirth and he has never found any other woman who is good enough to take her place.

Albin's father was also an upstanding man. It's really too bad that he died from illness before his time. He was the best advisor he has ever had. Back then, problems were easily resolved. Instead of wasting time waiting for various advisors to say something, Cai often used him as a sounding board. Between the two of them, they would fix the issues quickly regardless of the magnitude.

Without him, the Chief is stuck with a bunch of yes-men who are as useless as they come. Now that he thinks about it, maybe it's because he depended on him too much, which may have led the other advisors to become the way they are. If he has given them more of a voice back then, perhaps they can be a little bit more helpful now. Oh, well, there is no point drudging up the past. He will have to do something about them sometime soon, but there is something more pressing to consider right now.

The decision rests solely on the chief himself and he needs to make it quick. If he lets the stranger rot in the cell too much longer, he is likely to become disgruntled and does something evil just to get back at them. After weighing the pros and cons, he decides to give Gavin Anderson a chance, at least on a probationary basis. After all, he has a valid point.

He is only *one* man. He comes unarmed – if you don't count the ones that are necessary for survival. Perhaps, he can help teach the islanders better or faster techniques to build things. Or, at the very least, he can entertain the children with tales of his voyage.

Of course, there is always a flip side to everything. If he is as good as he claims, he may try to sabotage existing buildings without us knowing until it's too late. Or, he can try to brainwash the children. How easy would it be to sneak in a couple of propagandas into story time? Or, he may scare the children by telling them about cannibalism. Just to be safe, he is going to put a couple of guards on him to make sure that he does not try anything.

Of course, no one is happier about this decision than Fouke. After the guards give him the good news, he is overjoyed that he no longer has to room with the resident rodents. Now, he lives in a very small hut with a couple of very old widows. Because of their seniority on the island, nobody calls them by their actual names. Instead, they are simply known as Nonni and Grami. Cai figures he can help them around the house. Additionally, these ladies are very perceptive. If anyone can tell whether or not he is sincere in wanting to help, they can. If Anderson passes the test, maybe he can be upgraded with something better.

Now that the stranger is being dealt with, he is going to focus on the other obvious problem on the island – getting rid of the dead weight in his council. It is not going to be easy to find trustworthy people to replace them, but the first part will be. Since most of his advisors have no spine, they will not put up much of a fight, at least publicly.

Chapter 4: Amelia's Anguish

Back in Balavan, Violet is getting frustrated that no one seems to be able to find Fouke. Somehow, he looks as if to have disappeared overnight literally. Even the undercover agents who have been planted in the underground world have not been successful in finding a single reliable tip. Instead, they have been busy chasing after false leads. Perhaps, that is his plan all along. Because Fouke is such a master of disguise, he can be just about anyone. Hence, it's no surprise that thousands of tips flood the intelligence office in the Desiderios headquarters.

Unbeknownst to her, there is someone else on the lookout for the now infamous escapee – Amelia Richardson, Victor's supposed widow. Publicly, she is a very depressed widow, one who shies away from view because she can no longer bear life without her husband. Privately, she harbored a deep anger against the Desiderios and her own son, Thom.

Knowing that Fouke is the only one of her husband's men who never betrayed Victor and escaped, Amelia is eager to find him. Unlike Violet, however, she much better luck looking for him because she has something that the Desiderios don't – money, and lots of it. Although Thom was given ownership of Victor's entire fortune, Amelia still has a great deal of money hidden away. The only people who know about the existence of this sizeable fortune are Amelia and Victor. Everyone else, including their son, thinks the only thing she has left is her small country estate. Some, including her own son, wonders how she can even pay the servants who have followed her there. More than once, he has tried to send her money, but each time, it is returned to him immediately.

Using her secret stash, she has been able to pay people to find Fouke a lot faster than anyone else can. All she had to do to get someone is to ask around in the underground. Within days of Fouke's disappearance, she found a man who claims to have seen him making his boat in the dead of the night. This person also tells her which direction he headed. Having been married to the former Generalissimo, she has learned a thing or two about strategies. As soon as she hears of the tip, she knows immediately that the report is credible. If she were to escape from Balavan, she would also go in a direction that leads to the open sea. That way, no one can tell for sure where she is really going.

Before going after Fouke, however, Amelia has to getting ready first. Like any other mission in life, it is much easier if one goes in with a plan. The first thing she needs to do is recruit some trustworthy men. Where can she start? Obviously, she cannot just waltz into the underground and put up posters. This has to be done relatively stealthily. The best way to get back at anyone is by surprise.

Even though the Desiderios confiscated all of Victor's military records from the Legionnaire headquarters, Amelia still has his personal journals. He has kept one ever since he began his military career. Considering that he has such a high profile job, he has also kept the fact that he has journals secret from everyone except his wife.

Therefore, Amelia is pretty sure that he has written some highly sensitive information in them. Over time, there are about two dozen of them.

Amelia helped disguise their existence by putting on a fake book cover over them and putting them among novels that she has been reading in her personal library. After moving out of their mansion, she took the entire content of the library with her without arousing any suspicion from her son or the Desiderios.

Before his apparent *death*, she has never wanted to read them. With the respect that she had in him, she always felt like it would be an invasion of his privacy. Now that she thinks he is gone, it's about time she finds out what secrets he has been keeping in them. At the very least, she is hoping that there is something in them that can help her find a lead or a name of someone she can trust to lead this fight. As she flips through the earlier volumes, they are filled with entries of gallantry and how he wanted to push harder to rise through the ranks. He spoke about how he looked up to the general who was in charge at the time and wanted to be exactly like him. With perseverance and hard work, he steadily beat out hundreds of classmates in order to get promoted. She can tell from the tone of his writing that he was proud of his own achievements without explicitly saying so.

In between those entries are ones about her. He has not forgotten that a successful career means nothing without someone to share it with. Victor and Amelia met when they were still in grade school. They had been best friends before they fell in love with one another. As these entries attest, he had always loved her and never strayed from her from the minute he laid eyes on her. As she reads his tender words, tears flow through her eyes.

She misses him so much that she can actually feel her heart breaking. Wiping her eyes, she sits back up straight and is more determined than ever to avenge her soul mate.

As she continues to read deep into the night, she has completely forgotten about the time. Before long, she has fallen asleep on her couch with the journal over her face. It has been a while since she has had a decent night of sleep since she lost Victor. Hence, it is no surprise that she has not had a dream in a long time, either. But, not tonight. For the first time in months, she drifts into the dreamland.

It starts out as a colorful and beautiful dream. She is young and wearing an elegant bright red dress and walking towards a grand ball room filled with bright and elegant décor. As she gets closer, she can smell the perfume and see wall to wall covering of food and wine. The entire room is filled with hundreds of happy people. The men are all wearing military regalia and the women are all in their finest formal gowns. It looks like every one of them are walking arm in arm with their loved ones.

As she looks all around her, she cannot find her man. Then, she starts to panic. Where is Victor? He was here just a second ago, she tells herself in the dream. She goes to one couple and asks whether or not they have seen Victor. They shake their heads. She rushes from one couple to another asking them the same question. All of them have the same answer – no.

Finally, she sees her son, Thom. He is all alone on the side of the ball room. She walks up to him and asks if he has seen his father. Thom says yes, he has. Excited, she asks, "Where is he?"

Thom replies, "He cannot come out right now."

"Why not?" She asks with anticipation.

"He has been very bad and he is being punished."

"Tell me where?" she screams to him.

As she looks at him, he is saying something, but she cannot hear him. As she starts to ask again, she seems to be pulled away. It gets darker and darker. She keeps trying to reach for her son, but she is getting further and further away until all she can see is darkness. Suddenly, she shakes awake on her couch. Sweat is pouring down her face.

"He's alive!" Amelia exclaims.

She is sure of it. Even though it is just a dream, she firmly believes that Thom is trying to tell her that her beloved Victor is *not* dead, but he cannot tell her because he is bound to keep it a secret. Despite her recent anger towards her son, however, she knows that he can never lie to her if she asks him a direct question – even in a dream. She needs to get the truth from his mouth. She looks at the clock. It's 4AM – close enough. Oversleeping is never good for anybody.

She picks up the phone and looks for Thom's number, but cannot seem to find it. She never bothers to remember her son's number because she has programmed it into her phone. All she has to do to call him and say, "Call Son." After his betrayal, however, she immediately deleted all of his pertinent information. She does not ever want to see his name anywhere, least of all on something she has with her most of the time. Because she no longer recognizes him as her son, it now feels like a slap in the face to have to say those words.

After looking frantically through an old address book, she finally finds her phones numbers. When the phone rings, Thom wonders who in the world would be calling at this hour. As he looks at the phone, he cannot believe his eyes. He rubs them a little just to be sure that he is looking at it correctly. Yes, it's no mistake. It is his mother. At the instant, a part of him is very excited while other parts of him are a little terrified. While he is hoping against hope that she has forgiven him and wants to mend fences, he knows better.

Sitting up, he politely says, "Hello, mother, how are you?"

"I am not calling for any pleasantries."

His heart sinks upon hearing those words even though he has expected her to still be very upset.

She continues, "I want you to answer one question and I want you to tell me the truth."

Oh, oh. This cannot be good. He has never heard her so upset, and deadly serious, before.

"Is your father alive?"

Puzzled by the question, Thom says, "No, what makes you think he is?"

Then, holding back tears, she gathers as much nerves as she can and asks, "Did you watch his execution?"

After what seems like forever, Thom admits, "No."

"So, you don't know for sure that he is not alive."

"Mother, I know how much you want to believe that he is. I do, too.

Upon hearing those last three words, Amelia just about loses it. "How dare you?! You are the one *responsible* for what happened to him! How dare you pretend to care about him? He has done everything for you. Everything! You ungrateful little rat!"

"Guess it's too good to be true after all," Amelia says to herself as she hangs up the phone.

Cuddling into a ball on the corner of the couch, she starts sobbing again. For the first time since the end of the war, she lets herself cry for as long as she wants without holding back. She can no longer hold it in or pretend it does not hurt. She cannot remember the last time she has been so sad. Ever since she has known Victor, he has always made everything better, no matter the situation. And, there were many times when things went bad.

After she stops feeling sorry for herself, she returns to the journals. As she gets to more recent entries, she is back sitting up reading intently. Instead of reminiscing the old days, she is now back on her original mission – finding useful clues. Here is a curious entry from 26 years ago.

*

July 26, 2065

It's finally happened! Today, I am finally going to be promoted to the rank of General. Everyone who is anyone is going to be there to watch me at the ceremony at 2PM. I should be on the moon, but somehow I am not. I don't even know why. This is what I have been working toward my entire life. Why do I not feel more satisfied?

It's strange. I was much happier on my wedding day than today. Even though I have always known that Amelia is the love of my life, I was still excited knowing that she will be my wife from that day forward.

It should be just like this. I have always known I am going to be a general one day. I should be beyond ecstatic. I will be the leader of the Legionnaires from this day forward.

Oh, well, maybe it hasn't caught up with me yet. Perhaps if I give it time…

*

Amelia finds this entry a little strange, too. Victor has never mentioned his dissatisfaction with his career. He has always looked very content and comfortable in his position. He has never once complained about it. Well, at least she knows that he was excited about their marriage. Then, she reads an article that brings back more painful memories that she has been trying to get over for decades.

*

December 21, 2066

This has to be the saddest day I have ever had in my life. I feel so sorry for my dear wife. I cannot imagine what is going through her head right now. After having tried for so many years, our dear son was a stillborn. At least we had the chance to hold him and say goodbye. We do not have a name for him. It's just too painful to give him one right now. He will forever been known as our Baby Boy.

*

Amelia's head is now throbbing. She has spent many years trying to heal the wound. To stop the pain, she tried to forget her first born child, but how can she? Even though it has been a quarter of a century, she still remembers the exact moment she first saw his little angelic face. He was the most beautiful and perfect thing she has ever seen, but it was all an illusion. His lifeless body was so tiny and pale in her arms. She was wishing that he was simply asleep, even though she knew it was not true.

It was a very difficult time for both of them. Even though there was really nothing he could have done, Victor blamed himself for not having taken better care of his wife during her pregnancy. He told himself that he had worked too hard and didn't see the warning signs. The truth of the matter was that nobody could have seen them, because there weren't any.

When they first got married, having a child was something that they often talked about. Victor wanted a boy and a girl and Amelia wanted four children, but didn't care which kind. They frequently joked with one another about how a little Victor or a little Amelia would have gotten in trouble doing this or that. Those were the good days and they are long gone.

They started trying to have a child almost immediately after they were married, but it was not as easy as they thought. After seeing some specialists, the doctors were not optimistic about their chances, but encouraged them to try anyways.

They figured their love is strong enough to overcome any obstacle. They just need to believe in each other. As far as they are concerned, if it's meant to be, it will happen. After trying for nine years, she was extremely excited that she finally conceived.

It was nothing short of a miracle, which started out with a perfectly normal pregnancy. In fact, Amelia never felt better in her life. Those were one of the happiest eight months she has ever felt. It seemed that every day was a wonderful day, even when it was stormy or cloudy, nothing could get her down. She enjoyed every kick from the baby and she did not have any pains or other symptoms. The doctors had told them that the baby was perfectly healthy.

Three weeks before the due date, her water broke and she was rushed to the hospital. Even then, the doctors have told her that everything is going well. The baby was a little small, but perfectly normal. There is nothing to worry about. It wasn't until the baby was about to be born did the doctors realize that something terrible is happening. The umbilical cord was wrapped tightly around the baby's neck and he had been without oxygen for more than twenty minutes. Although the doctors tried to save the baby, it was too late.

That day, both Victor and Amelia's lives changed forever. Even though on the surface, Victor tried to be the same loving husband that he had always been, Amelia can tell that he was becoming a different person. He was more serious and stern. Even though he was never one to share his emotions, he was becoming more distant.

At the time, Amelia excused his changed behavior to that of more responsibility at work, but she knew the real reason. He was trying to hide from it all. Coming home to the empty baby's room was too difficult for him. He was also ashamed of facing his wife, even though he had no reason to. Nevertheless, he made a point of being there for his wife on special occasions. That was when he began to buy extravagant gifts and hold elaborate parties. It was apparently the only way he knew how to cope with his son's death.

Looking at the ground, Amelia thinks, "He would have been 25 years old this year. I wonder what kind of man he would have turned out to be." Before a tear can drop out of her eye, anger returns as she thinks of Thom. "I am sure he would not have betrayed his own father."

Returning to the journal, she can tell that the anger is written on the pages after that day. Even the handwriting has changed somewhat. Instead of the calm, gentle penmanship, the letters are more pronounced as if he was pushing the pen harder on the pages to take out anger. For most of the next volume, it is filled entirely with writings about work. He no longer mentioned his love for his wife or anything about his personal life for that matter. Then, she comes across another interesting entry.

*

May 2, 2068

The troops are getting restless. I have got to do something before a mutiny starts. Life has been too easy on them. It's time to test them and see what they are made out of before they turn into mush.

*

Amelia has never thought that Victor would be afraid of a mutiny. He seemed to always been in full control of everything that is going on. In fact, he always got what he wanted. If he wanted a law to be passed, it happened. If he wanted someone to be in his army, he was enlisted the very next day.

But, that would explain why there were so many campaigns going starting about that time. The Legionnaires seemed to be fighting in one battle after another. It was always somewhere far away. So much so that people in Balavan didn't really care about them. The only things they knew were the large amount of booty the men would carry with them when they returned.

She never asked why Victor felt a need to pick a fight with the neighboring dominions. He never bothered to explain. He would simply tell her that it was a military necessity to keep us safe. At least, now she knows what he meant. It wasn't Balavan that he was talking about; it was his hold on the Legion as a whole. If his men did rebel against him, their lives would definitely have been in danger.

*

September 20, 2072

I didn't think this day was ever going to come. Amelia and I are finally parents! Thom was born this morning at 7:05 AM. He is 21 inches long and weighs a healthy 7 pounds 11 ounces. We couldn't be prouder!

*

Even though it is only a short blurb, this is the first entry that Victor has written in years that does not have to do with work. She is surprised to see how happy he sounded when he wrote about this event in his journal. Yes, that was the day that they went to the hospital to pick up their newly adopted baby boy. They named him Thom.

It was a bittersweet day for both of them. It was a miracle, but Amelia could not hide her sorrow. She wished that she was giving birth to him rather than watching him be born. His birth mother was a scared teenage girl who could not take care of him. Like a classic tale of cowardice, her boyfriend had left her when he found out that she was carrying a child and her parents have kicked her out of the house. Alone and penniless, she had no other choice but to give him up.

Like the pregnancy itself, this adoption was not exactly planned. By then, Amelia was already 39 years old and Victor was 40. The chance of her conceiving is almost none, especially considering how long it took her to conceive the first time around. After sidestepping the subject for years, Victor finally decided to see a doctor just to see if there is even a chance it could ever happen.

At the hospital, he met Thom's biological mother who was crying and shivering like a leaf in the waiting room. He went over to talk with her and found out about her predicament. He had offered to pay for her medical expenses, which she was very grateful to receive, but she was still terrified because she did not know how to care for the infant when he came.

She had not finished school and had no real job. She had been living with friends who were nice enough to let her crash in their place for the time being, but she knew that her welcome was wearing thin. It was only meant to be a temporary thing until the baby came. After that, she didn't know where she would go or live. After seeing a counselor, she had decided that the best thing to do was to give the child up for adoption.

Right there and then, Victor offered to adopt the child from her on the condition that she must never reveal her identity to anyone else nor claim the child any time after the birth. She agreed. He had not even thought about what his wife would say. As expected, when Amelia first heard about the adoption, she was also shaking like a leaf. She didn't know how to feel. On one hand, she was angry that her husband never discussed the possibility before making such a life changing decision on his own. On the other, she was scared. She had wanted a child so badly, but never thought one would just show up like that. It took for some time, but soon, she was excited about the idea.

As far as anyone besides the hospital staff is concerned, Thom was the biological child of Amelia and Victor. To keep up the charade, Amelia wore loose clothing for months since finding out about the adoption to give the illusion that she was with child. When they came home with Thom, no one had ever questioned that Amelia had given birth, not even the maids and the servants who had been living with them for years.

On the day that Thom was born, Amelia had made a promise that she would take care of him as her own and would cherish him with every ounce of her body. Although Thom may not think so, she has done everything possible for him, even though every time she looks at him, she feels an emptiness that just will not go away. After having made so much effort, she just cannot believe how things have turned out for them.

Chapter 5: Victor's Clues

It's now morning. Amelia looks out the window, it is a glorious day. Too bad the weather does not match how she feels inside. Still in her bathrobe, she goes to the kitchen to get a cup of coffee. As the maid is about to add a heaping spoonful of creamer and sugar in it like the way she is used to taking them, Amelia takes out her hand and says, "No, I am good," as she takes the cup of black coffee from her.

Surprised at the request, the maid wonders if Amelia is turning over a new leaf or trying to open a new chapter in her life. If she is, that may be a good thing. She has been quite depressed lately and the servants are beginning to really worry about her, but no one dares to inquire. If they simply do as they are told, they are rewarded with lavish gifts and handsome paychecks.

On the other hand, if they pry or disobey, they face harsh consequences in the form of termination, docked pay, or removal of any form of privileges such as the use of her cars or eating of her food. Hence, in the Richardson household, the hired help do not ask questions if they know what is good for them.

Nevertheless, they can clearly see that something is just not right. Amelia has asked to be alone for months, long before she began reading the journals in the library. There are days when she would sit alone in the dark for hours. Often, when the servants knock on the door for meal time, she simply says, "Leave it at the door" and take her meals in her room. Sometimes, the tray would still be full.

Today, the maid also notices two more unexpected oddities with her boss. First, Amelia has not changed her clothes. It's not like her to walk around the house without looking like she is ready to go out on town no matter what time of the hour it is.

Being the wife of the Generalissimo, there were always unexpected visitors who would come unannounced. Hence, she had always been ready no matter who might show up at her doorstep. Everything from her hair, makeup, outfit, jewelry, accessories, and shoes are always the top of the line and in perfect condition.

Second, the maid is amazed at how good she looks au natural. Now that she lives in the outskirt of town and believes she is a widow, she no longer cares what she looks like in the comfort of her own home. Ironically, she looks better without all of those cosmetics on her face. Now, she looks refreshing and clean. At 58 years old, she still looks pretty great for her age.

After getting her morning caffeine, Amelia returns to her couch in silence to continue her reading with the door closed. Meanwhile, the maid goes back to preparing breakfast like she does every day without saying a word.

After reading so many volumes of the journal, Amelia is about to give up finding anything useful. Every time there is an entry about work, it is usually too generic. He almost never uses actual names. Instead, he would refer to people only as a unit or by rank. Perhaps, he did not want to single anyone out or it could also be that he didn't know what their names were.

Being at his level, it must be difficult to remember names of each individual. In his more recent volumes, however, he has dropped a few names, like this entry.

*

September 20, 2091

There is a new recruit today. His name is Russell. I believe he has potential. Only time will tell.

*

It's strange that Victor would single out a recruit with such a short entry. There is really nothing in the writing that raises a flag, but it's not what is in it that piques Amelia's interest. It's what isn't.

Why would the great Generalissimo mention him without any details? Who is he? What makes him so special? How did he find him? What can he do for them that the rest of the Legionnaires cannot?

After all, this entry was written only a month before the war ended. It almost seemed like he was Victor's final chance to turn the tide. Since the Legion lost, Victor's hope was obviously misplaced, but this Russell is definitely still very intriguing.

Perhaps, he was not given enough time to prove himself. Amelia puts a small bookmark on it so she can be sure to go back to it later.

Then, she flips back to see if there are any mentions of Thom when he was recruited.

"Let's see, when did that little man join the Legionnaires? Was it 2085 or 2086." Amelia tries to remember.

Perusing through the pages from early 2085, she sees nothing about Thom, but does see some references of the war, which makes perfect sense. After all, the war started that year. Then, she sees some mention of El Diablo and the Warrior.

*

November 13, 2085

Cannot believe the enemy has such a resilient man on as a leader. If rumors are true, this El Diablo fellow must be one brave young man. He puts some real fear in my men. Wonder what would it take to appease him? It would be great if I can recruit men like that. Or better, recruit him. Yeah, that would be the day.

I hear he also has a pretty good partner next to him – this Warrior. What a name these two have. I hear that she is every bit as fierce as he is. I definitely need more men like them. Time to recruit some fresh blood.

*

Interesting, Victor seems to be admiring his enemies. That cannot be good. No wonder he lost! How can anyone plan on winning a war if he has so much respect for the opposite team? It sounds like his morale took a sharp dive sometime over the past few years.

He had no intention on winning. Then, a thought comes to her mind that puts a faint smile back on her face. So, her man is a true team player. Even when his heart is not in it, he can still hold on to a fight for six long years.

As she continues to flip, she sees a little blurb about the recruits.

*

May 6, 2086

Sending some of my best young men to rally fresh recruits from some of the local schools today. I need people with heart and soul, and not just meatheads. Have enough of them already.

I think the boys would make an excellent addition to my team. They both have their own strengths, but separate, neither one of them can accomplish much. One has the brains but no heart and the other is just the opposite. Together, however, they can be my new secret weapon.

*

That's right. That's about the time that they visited Thom and Max's school. Although he never mentions either one of them by name, Amelia is sure those are the boys that Victor was referring to. Who else can they be? Everyone knows that Max was the smartest student in school. He was always well ahead of the rest of the classes.

Thom, on the other hand, was Mr. Popular. Every girl in school loved him. He was charming and athletic. He definitely had spirit and was always eager to help out.

On the other hand, if they are such a dynamic due, why would Victor not mention them by name? Was Victor embarrassed by them? He didn't have a reason to. Was he afraid to put their names down in fear that they may be targeted if the enemy got their hands on the journal? This is a possibility, but remote considering that no one besides the two of them even knows the existence of the journals.

In either case, this Russell boy must be something special if he gets an actual name written in the journal if neither Thom nor Max did despite being referred to as his "new secret weapon." Amelia is more determined than ever now to find this boy. Searching for more clues, she comes across the following entry.

*

October 2, 2091

I hope I am wrong, but I am really concerned that I may be losing him, too, my dear boy. After all that I have done for him, I cannot believe he is going to betray me, just like his friend. Where did I go wrong? I know I may seem a little distant at times, but he always seemed quite happy with me. Why would he do something like this to me?

I have no choice but to send a rescue mission. I don't know if he can do anything, but I hope Russell can turn him around. He is my last chance.

*

Well, this entry is quite obvious. His *dear boy* can be no one but Thom. Amelia knew that Max had gone missing, but she had always thought that the Desiderios kidnapped him. From this entry, it sounds like he defected on his own. Victor had never mentioned the possibility to her before. Maybe, he was trying to protect her by not mentioning such things.

From his tone of voice, it sounds pretty clear that Victor thought Thom also defected. Yet, he didn't do anything to stop him. He even gave him the benefit of the doubt by sending someone to try to change his mind. He obviously

54

still loved his son very much. Ironic, even though Thom was the one with the heart, he seemed to be the weak one in the end. After all, no strong willed general can change sides so easily, not the least the second in command.

Then, Amelia flips to the last page. She almost dreads to see what is in it.

*

October 16, 2091

Just got intel that things have gone terribly wrong. Amelia, my love, I may never see you again. Don't you ever doubt my love for you! I tried my best with our boy, but it was not meant to be.

Do you remember our first date? I will always cherish it. If I were to be anywhere with you, I would go back to where we went that day. It was so magical!

*

Amelia's hands are shaking as she read this final entry. She is very excited about what she has read, yet scared at the same time. It's almost like his farewell note to her, but she is not sure what to think. It is like a love letter, but not really. He is definitely trying to tell her something without spelling it out. There is only one way to find out. One thing she is sure about – this is the first clue that she has been looking for.

Victor obviously wants her to go to the location where they had their first date. He must have left some more clues for her there for her to follow. It makes perfect sense. If he is careful enough not to divulge too much information in a secret journal, he is also not going to give away everything in one place, either.

Putting the journals away, she quickly gets dressed. Trying to stay inconspicuous, she looks for as plain of an outfit in as muted of a color as she can possibly find in her wardrobe collection. Although everything she has is made of fine silk or cashmere, she chooses a plain white shirt, a pair of black slacks, and a simple pair of ballet flats. She forgoes all jewelry. Normally, she hates such a homey look, but she is quite proud of it today.

Then, she instructs the servants not to disturb her before sneaking out the back door. Yes, it feels strange for the lady of the house to have to slip out of her own house like a common burglar, but it cannot be helped. It's better to be overly careful and keep all of this to herself than to risk being discovered by anyone.

There is no telling if she is being watched or if there is already a spy amongst her own household. Naturally, she takes one of the maid's car that is parked in the back on the field rather than her usual climate controlled limousine out front.

She cannot have anyone follow her in case there is something there that Victor does not want anyone else to see or hear.

As she drives cautiously to her destination, her heart is racing. It was so many decades ago and she has not been back there in a very long time. She wonders if it is still the same as she remembers it. Just the thought of her first date makes her smile.

They were so young and innocent then. Everything was wonderful. There was not a care in the world besides one another.

After about an hour, she has finally arrived – their old school playground. Since the beginning of the war, the school has been abandoned in favor of another one that is towards the outskirts of town. During the war, it has suffered quite a bit of damage. The school superintendent has decided not to return to it.

Instead, the new sovereign Garret has decided to demolish it the following month so they can turn it into a large public park and arboretum. Considering the devastation over the last six years, it is time to replace depleted and damaged structures around Balavan with something beautiful.

Amelia would hate to see this place go. This is where little Victor and Amelia had their first play date during recess. They were both ten years old. Victor had brought extra brownies he saved from the previous night's dinner to share with his childhood sweetheart. Even though they were both very young, they knew that they were meant for one another.

She walks towards a large oak tree where they both sat down to enjoy their treat. It has gotten much larger than she remembers. She looks around for any signs from Victors, but hasn't found anything obvious, which she has expected. If it was too easy to find, it would not have been left by Victor.

She touches the bark and remembers the day that Victor carved a heart with their initials on it. Yes, it was not a nice thing to do to the tree, but it was a very romantic gesture, especially back then. She is certain that she is touching the right spot, but she no longer sees it. Then, she shakes her head and realizes how silly she is to think it hasn't moved as the tree grows. She looks up a few feet higher and there it is.

As she looks at the marking, she notices that the plus sign looks a little odd. After studying it, this part looks like it was carved later than the rest and looks more like an arrow now. She looks in the direction of the arrow; she sees a see-saw. She remembers it fondly. She would leap on the see-saw while Victor was on the other end, just to see if he would fall off. Yes, in hindsight, it was another thing that was not nice to do, but being the man he was, he never fell nor showed any fear.

Sitting on the see-saw, she is saddened that he is not on the other end. Then, she spots some graffiti that has been written on the pavement next to her. It has drawings of palm trees, various flowers, tanks, guns, and several words spread across the entire drawing, all in dramatic colors. Although some of the paint has chipped and parts of the pavement have cracked or are missing from the shelling, she can still make out the words. Reading from the top to bottom, she makes out "Car," "Victory," "Peace," "Son," and "Love" intermingled in the artwork.

Is this the message that Victor is trying to give her? What does it mean? Amelia wonders. Separately, every one of those five words is items that everyone in Balavan wants. Hence, they certainly sound generic enough to just be the rambling of a frustrated artist who is trying to put his anger on his canvas. To a normal passerby, it certainly would not attract too much undue attention.

If Victor actually wrote this or commissioned someone to, what is he trying to say? He obviously would have had it written before the war ended, but by the time he wrote that last entry, Victor pretty much already knew that the Legionnaires would not have a victory even though the city itself would have achieved some form of peace after the war. On the other hand, the Legionnaires did have quite a few material possessions like cars. Some, like Victor himself, have sons and love.

Hm, Amelia is an intelligent woman, but is somewhat baffled. Is a car the key to victory and peace? If so, which car? Is it their son's? Is the clue in Thom's car? After thinking about the possibility for a minute, Amelia decides that it is not likely. By then, Victor already suspected that

Thom would betray him. Why would he put a clue in a traitor's vehicle for his wife to find? It is simply too risky. Knowing Victor the way Amelia does, he would not put her in any sort of danger.

Trying to rearrange the words a little, she wonders what else this message can mean. After pondering for another while, a thought suddenly comes to her. Maybe it's a name! If you put the words "car" and "son" together, you get Carson. Isn't that the name of the murdered sovereign? Then again, David Carson was a corrupt man. Why would Victor think that Caron would lead to victory with love and peace?

Unless, he was not referring to *that* Carson. As far as most people know, including Amelia, Carson died without having any children, at least not legitimate ones. On the other hand, perhaps he had a secret love child somewhere. That can help explain why Victor would put the words "son" and "love" together. While "peace" and "victory" work hand in hand, those two words do not. Why not? It makes perfect sense! Victory wouldn't create a clue that is too difficult to decipher. He knew that she is not trained in espionage.

Nevertheless, it's probably better not to speculate. After all, it is not that unusual of a surname. There may be thousands of people in Balavan with that name. She stared one last time to commit it to memory. Amelia does not want to take a photograph of any kind to avoid arousing curiosity from any potential by passers. Then, she hurries home before the maids suspect anything.

*

Going back to what she knows best, she immediately gets on the special phone that she has bought just for this purpose. With a push of a button, she is speaking with Scout, the person who has been able to get her any information she asks – for the right price. There are days when she cringes a little when speaking with this seemingly unlimited source of knowledge that is so willing to give up information.

A small part of her is somewhat uneasy about the mysterious relationship that they have together. She is fully aware that Scout is nothing more than an alias. When introducing one another, she called herself Mrs. Jones, which is just as well. Besides these obviously fictitious labels, they know next to nothing about the other party. In fact, Amelia is not even sure if this Scout is a man or a woman. She wants to say it's a man with a high monotone voice. Even though the reception is clear, the phone seems to have a voice changer on it. She is also pretty sure that it is untraceable.

It is pretty clear that neither party trusts the other. Why would they? Being in the dirt gathering business, Scout depends on anonymity to get the job down. He can be anyone at any time, the waiter at the diner, the bus driver, the school teacher, the homeless man, the police officer, or even a servant.

"What if he has infiltrated her home and pretends to be one of her hired help?" Amelia ponders in a panic. Then again, she has not hired anyone new in the past three years. Since she personally is no one special and leads such a seemingly dull life, she convinces herself that there is no way anyone can lie low in her household for so long. Chuckling a little, she figures that it would be considered a slow form of torture that no one should have to endure.

Meanwhile, Amelia has no intention of letting anyone know that she is not the mourning depressed widow that she pretends to be. So far, she has kept all conversation to a strictly business level. She does not even waste any time with idle chatter. She never gives any form greetings or gives away any information such as mentioning the weather. She figures this is a good way to keep a nice distance between the two. As far as she is concerned, no business relationship ever ends well if emotions are attached.

Even though Scout is not as frigid as Amelia, he also has no desire to reveal his true identify. As long as money is exchanged as promised and the information is delivered on time, they are both very happy with their arrangements.

"Scout, I need some information on Carson," Amelia says immediately without even announcing who she is.

"Ah, Mrs. Jones. Good to hear from you again."

"When can you get it for me?" Amelia continues, completely ignoring the greeting.

"Are you referring to our poor deceased former sovereign or someone else?"

"Both."

"Please be more specific."

"I want to know if David Carson has any illegitimate children, nephew, nieces, siblings, or anyone else who is between the ages of 15 and 45."

"Understood."

"When will I have it?" Amelia repeats her question impatiently.

"Next week. Same time. Same place. Same fee."

With that, Amelia hangs up the phone. For the first time since being alone, she has a good feeling about this.

Chapter 6: New Confidants

After hiding out on Trozos Island for about a month, Fouke is completely cut off from the rest of the world, just the way Chief Cai likes it. He has no idea that Amelia is looking for him. Instead, he is starting to get the hang of things and actually trying to start a brand new life.

It can be a little difficult for him at times because his pride would always come back, but he has managed to get a hold of himself and not show that part of him to anyone else. So far, he is very happy with the results. Despite the fact that he is being watched 24 hours a day, the people there are generally very nice to him.

Even Nonni and Grami, the old widows who were initially very suspicious of him, have taken a real liking to him. Being at the top of his game, he has agreed to help out with everything any time anyone asks. He has fixed so much broken furniture, taught so many children, and done so many odd jobs around the island that he has lost count.

His body shows it, too. His hands are filled with callouses and his arms and face have scrapes and cuts from working all day and all night. Yet, he always manages to keep a smile on his face, which is very difficult to do considering that he can care less about these people if they did not own this island. His acting is so convincing that, on occasion, some of the islanders actually feel sorry for him and offer to help, making it easier for him to pass the days.

In a way, it's like a prison sentence. He is hoping to be let out early for good behavior. He knows that it takes time to change people's attitude towards him, but once it's changed, it will be smooth sailing for him. At least, that is what he is hoping. With the way things are going, the chief will soon be comfortable enough to let him go anywhere unsupervised. Until then, he will not change a thing. He just needs to be patient enough to wait it out.

Watching his progress, Albin is glad that he has convinced the chief to give Gavin a chance. He feels like he has helped contribute to the island as whole by giving the people a reliable helper. Meanwhile, Nimue does not have much to say. She keeps to herself. Secretly, she is wondering if she has been wrong about this new intruder.

*

Meanwhile, back in Balavan, Scout has gathered the information that Amelia has been waiting for. Being a very rigid person, he, or at least Amelia would like to think it's a he, likes to follow the rules to a fault, but he also knows how much his employer wants this information. One of his golden rules is to keep a happy customer above all things. So, here goes nothing.

Calling Amelia a day early, Scout asks, "Do you want to know now or wait until our agreed upon day?"

"What kind of question is that?" Amelia says in anticipation.

Of course, she wants it now. Why would she want to wait a single second longer? What a silly question.

"David Carson was an only child. His parents were faithful to one another. So, there are no illegitimate siblings, either. So, there are no nephews or nieces to speak of. David himself, however, was not nearly as discreet. He was connected to at least five women, despite never marrying any of them. Out of these five, there are three children who may be David's based on the time that they were together."

Scout pauses for a moment for Amelia to interject. She always has questions, but not this time. All she does is nod over the phone as she listens intensely.

"The first one is a girl named Iris. She is 28 years old. Like her father, she can be bought at any price. She has no one place she calls home. So, nobody really knows where she lives or where she is at any one time. The second is a boy named Owen. He is 23 and a school teacher. He has been working at the same school teaching third graders for the last few years. The youngest one is another boy named Russell."

"Russell?" Amelia says immediately upon hearing that name.

"Yes, is there something specific you want to know about this one?"

"No, please continue."

"He is 19 years old and currently lives underground. He became a member of the Legionnaires a few weeks before the war ended."

Ah, so that's the connection! Amelia says to herself. This Russell is the Car and the Son that Victor was trying to tell her. She must find him.

"I need to see this Russell Carson," Amelia says.

Smiling, Scout says, "It's not Russell Carson."

Surprised, Amelia replies, "I thought you said its Carson's son."

Shaking his head in disbelief, Scout says, "There is a reason that nobody knows he is David's son. If he goes by his father's last name, it would be too easy to connect the dots."

Tapping herself on the head, Amelia says "Duh" and asks, "What is his real name?"

"He goes by his mother's maiden name. It's Russell Angleton."

"What do you know about him?"

"He was very close to his father in secret. He knows everything there is to know about the corruption and the payoffs that his father had. He also knows his father's best connections."

"Interesting. What about his mother?"

"What about her? She doesn't know anything. She doesn't even know that Russell has been seeing his father. Once he turned 18, he left home. As far as she is concerned, he is studying in some university outside of Balavan."

Amelia is now more intrigued than before about this young man. There are so many questions she wants answered. What is he up to? What did he do for David? Why did he not prevent his father's assassination? Before she can finish her thoughts, Scout asks "Where and when?" without missing a beat.

After discussing the logistics of it all, Amelia is so excited that she is finally getting somewhere. Now, she can put her husband's plan into action. Maybe she can avenge him now. Unlike Scout, she is willing to expose her identity to meet this young man. While Scout is somewhat surprised, she follows her orders without asking any questions.

*

The next few days, Amelia waits patiently for her meeting with the golden boy Russell Angleton. After her initial excitement is over, she tries to calm herself down. She knows that she is setting herself up for a disappointment if her expectations are too high. After all, he is merely a boy.

What in the world can a 19 year old do that her dear old husband couldn't?

Not letting her curiosity get the best of her, she distracts herself by reading and rereading her husband's journals, familiarizing herself with the concerns of the Generalissimo. Being his wife for so many decades, she is well aware of his etiquette and demeanor, but he had always kept work to himself. She needs to show this young man that she is as concerned about the causes of the Legionnaire as Victor. In turn, that would prove that she is as much of a leader as her husband in order to get his loyalty.

As the morning of the meeting finally rolls around, Amelia is more than ready. As previously agreed, she is to wear a blue outfit complete with a blue hat. He is to wear a solid blue shirt and black slacks. Having planned out what she wants to do, she puts on her finest clothes of the appropriate color, but opts for some understated jewelry to show that she is more professional than just a trophy wife.

Instead of getting a chauffeur, she decides to drive herself, but instead of a beat up car that she borrowed on her last trip out of town, she chooses one of her own luxury models.

Although they have agreed to meet for breakfast at 7:30AM in a crowded little place in downtown, she arrives at exactly 7AM, but sits in her car from across to street to watch the patrons go in and out of the restaurant. She is hoping to get a glimpse of him before they formally meet so she can get her first impression in before he speaks. She always finds it easier to get a good assessment of a person when he does not realize that he is being watched.

Unbeknownst to her, Russell is already there enjoying his breakfast. Even though he is only 19 years old, he has learned a great deal from his father and siblings. Instead of hiding in a luxury car, which is not as incognito as Amelia thinks it is, he is merely sitting in the corner table inside the restaurant. Apparently, the best hiding place is in plain sight. The key is to be there before you are expected to be.

After finishing his food, it is exactly 7:29AM. He pays for his meal and calmly walks towards her car. Upon seeing a young man fitting that description coming towards her, Amelia is taken by surprise. At first, she is a little shaken, but soon realizes that this is a *good* thing. He opens the passenger seat and gets in.

"Hello, Mrs. Richardson. I am Russell. It's an absolute honor to finally meet you," he says as he smiles and extends his hand to shake hers.

Smiling back, Amelia says, "I guess I don't need to introduce myself. How do you know who I am?"

"How can I not? You were the First Lady of Balavan," Russell replies with a grin.

Blushing a little, Amelia is glad that someone recognizes her as someone other than a depressed old woman. She is already impressed that he knows where she is without her getting out of her car. Guess all of that preparation is not really necessary. He seems to already be on board without her ever having to say anything, which begs the question, why?

Regardless of the answer, they cannot stay in the car forever. As she begins to drive back to her home, Russell asks, "Where to?"

"I am not sure," Amelia responds. She seems to be on automatic pilot, not even thinking where she is really headed.

"I don't think it's a good idea to head back to your country home," Russell replies as if he can also read her mind.

Nodding, Amelia says, "You are probably right."

"Do you mind if I drive?" Russell asks politely.

Normally, Amelia's immediate answer would not just be "No," but she couldn't help but feel like she wanted to trust him a little, so she agreed.

As he points his finger, Russell then says, "Can you just turn here?" After a minute, he says, "Stop right there by the curb."

Although Amelia is still eager to trust her new best friend and confidant, she is not sure why he is stopping in such a shady area.

Sensing her hesitation, he says, "Don't worry. This is our land."

For a split second, Amelia is actually panicking. Our land? Is he a part of a *gang*? She certainly hopes not, but she cannot help but wonder.

Is he going to rob her? Worse, if he going to *kill* her? What if he is a part of an underground guerrilla group? If so, there is no telling what his *real* agenda is. Just because they may be against the Desiderios, it does not mean that they are pro-Legion, either.

She really doesn't know anything about this young man except for a few words on a journal and clues that she *thinks* she has. What if she is wrong? Taking a deep breath, Amelia tells herself not to chicken out now. She must have faith in what she is doing or all is lost.

Even though Russell can read her face like an open book, he does not question her. It would only put her on the spot and possibly on the defensive, which would not be good for their new working relationship. He knows that he needs to give her something to ease her mind, but not now — soon.

"We are switching cars. It's just down the street," Russell continues.

Now, Amelia's nerves are really getting to her. Down the street? That's not a street, but a dark alley. It's like a bad nightmare from a movie – a wealthy woman being lured into a trap. She didn't even bring any sort of a weapon, not that it would be of any use to her.

Ironically, even though Victor was a military man, he was not a big fan of guns. Perhaps, it's because he has seen too much blood and violence to last him a life time and he has no desire to see more in the comfort of his own home. Or, he just didn't trust her with one in fear that she would hurt herself or a loved one. It's too late to learn how to use one now.

Praying that she makes it out of this alive, she isn't even aware that she is now holding her breath.

Russell can tell that if she keeps it up, she is going to pass out. Even though she is a relatively small woman, he has no desire to carry her the rest of the way.

"Are you alright?" he asks as he stops in his track.

Looking around for possible ambush, she nods.

"I promise I will not let anyone hurt you."

She nods again.

"It's OK. I am here to help. What do I need to do for you to trust me?"

"I trust you," she whispers.

Laughing, he says, "If you don't want to do this today. It's OK. We can go back to your car and do this some other time."

Shaking her head, "No, no. I want to. Let's go."

After walking around the corner, there is a small inconspicuous black car. There must be a few thousand cars in town that looks just like it. It's not old and decrepit like the one that her maid has and it's definitely not fancy like hers. There is nothing identifiable about it. There is nothing hanging from the rear view mirror, no stickers, no dents, no special license plate, and no objects viewable from the window. In addition, it is also not dirty or particularly clean.

"Here we are," Russell says.

As she hesitantly gets in the car, Russell say, "I apologize for taking you into this shady part of town. It cannot be helped. I cannot risk letting anyone know that we are working together. Since no one in this area drives a nice vehicle like yours, it's best that we are not seen in it any more than we need to."

"I know," Amelia says as she starts to calm down a little.

"Before we go out into public view, do you mind taking off your hat and put this brunette wig on instead?"

Nodding, Amelia obeys immediately as she tucks in her beautiful flowing blond hair into a knot.

"Also, please put on these sunglasses."

Nodding again, Amelia keeps looking out the window to see where they are as he takes off.

"We are going to our hideout," Russell says as if he can read her mind.

Nodding, Amelia remains silent for the rest of the trip, which seems to be taking an eternity.

*

Looking at her watch, they have been driving for about an hour, but she has no idea where. There is good reason for that. Instead of taking the shortest and most direct route, Russell takes a few detours and turns through some busy streets to throw off the scent of anyone who may be following them. When they finally arrive at a an empty field, Amelia looks at Russell in confusion.

"Where are we?"

Russell smiled at her and just wordlessly took her by her arm and led her into the woods.

There was a small, almost unused path that led into the woods. They went further and further until she felt like they were walking downwards.

Abruptly, the trail ended with a wall of bushes and shrubbery, but Russell kept going. Amelia followed him into the shrubs and behind it was another empty field.

Russell leaned down, and right behind the shrubs, he felt around on the ground and then abruptly pulled up a trapdoor.

Amelia gasped. She hadn't even seen it.

They descended into a large hallway that led to a single door. The walls of the hallway were made of rock, like it was carved out of a mountain. Russell opened it and gestured for her to enter.

To her surprise, she found a group of men and women there, all are heavily armed. Terrified, Amelia stands next to the door and does not move a muscle. They look like possible enemies.

"Please make yourself at home," Russell says as he points towards a sofa in the middle of the room.

"No, thank you. I am good here," Amelia replies.

"Well, Russell, I don't know what you did, but you scared the crap out of her, didn't you?" a woman says.

"No, I didn't. I only did what I had to in order to get here without being noticed."

Looking at everyone, Amelia wonders where she is.

"Everyone, I want you to meet Mrs. Victor Richardson," Russell announces.

Immediately, there is a thunder of clapping and cheering. Surprised, Amelia looks dumbfounded. While she has expected Victor to give her someone to work with, she never imaged that it is an entire group of eager young men and women.

"So, what is your command, Madame General?" Russell asks.

Madame General? What an interesting name. Being married to the former Generalissimo, she figures they may call her First Lady of Legionnaires or something on that line of thought, but she likes it. Guess she has become an honorary general despite the fact that she has no military training or experience. It's strange, but the dominant thought in her mind is that she hopes she will not disappoint them.

"Wow, I am speechless right now, which almost never happens" Amelia jokes as she laughs at herself. "You all will have to excuse me, but I have not expected all of this. I am going to have to get back with you on such a grandiose plan."

Nodding and laughing, a woman says, "Take your time. Meanwhile, would you like to be introduced to your new team members? I know we are not nearly as big as the Legion, but we are definitely doing our best."

"Of course. I understand," Amelia replies.

Extending her hand, the woman says, "Hi, I am Iris. I am Russell's sister."

Recognizing the name from Scout's report, Amelia smiles and says, "It's a pleasure to meet you."

"Do you recognize me?" Iris asks.

Looking at the young woman carefully, Amelia cannot recall having ever met her before. Usually, she is very good with names and faces. If they have met, even if it has been several years, she would have recognized her, at least a little.

Shaking her head, she says, "No, have we met?"

"Nope, but you may recognize my voice," Iris says with a grin.

Voice? Iris has a gentle feminine voice, but nothing really stands out. She has heard voices like that before. Somewhat embarrassed, Amelia is trying her hardest to try to place this young woman somewhere in her memory, but nothing comes up the top of her head. She thinks about everyone she has worked with and those who she may have been introduced to very briefly, but still she comes up with nothing.

"I am sorry, I don't know your voice, either."

Taking out a device, Iris puts it on her throat and says, "How about now?"

Surprised, Amelia looks like a deer in the headlight. Now, that is a voice that she can easily identify.

"You... You are Scout!" she exclaims.

"Bravo! You've got it!"

"It was you who I have been working with all of this time?"

"Yes, Madame! I hope you have been happy with my service."

"Very much so!" Amelia says. After a few seconds, she says, "Wait a minute, you told me about Iris in third person. You make her sound like a mystery woman whom nobody knows. Were you trying to throw me off of your scent?"

"Well, I cannot exactly reveal myself to you so haphazardly. The timing has to be right or you may not believe me. Besides, even though we had a pretty good idea that it was you, we could not be 100% sure until we have actually seen you. You did go by the alias Mrs. Jones instead of your real name. Because you prefer to remain behind the scenes during the war, it makes it that much more difficult for us to positively identify you any other way."

Nodding, Amelia cheerfully says, "Good point!"

It seems that when Amelia was asking around in the underground for information, Iris quickly spotted her. To keep the relatively naïve rich widow from asking the wrong people, she instantly volunteered her services.

Iris points over to another member of the team and says, "You may also recognize him. This is my other brother Owen."

"Oh, yes, the school teacher," Amelia replies with a smile. "It's a pleasure."

So, the entire Carson family is here. The late sovereign must have been a huge fan of Victor and the feeling is probably mutual. Otherwise, how can you explain why all three illegitimate children who have always stayed in the shadows have joined forces on Victor's side?

Owen smiles sheepishly as he says, "The pleasure is all mine" as he stares at the ground after their eyes met ever so briefly.

It's as if he has met a celebrity, which is actually not that far from the truth. The fact of the matter is he is a big admirer of the Richardsons, not just Victor. He has been a huge fan of Thom as well. Being a school teacher, he has studied Thom's techniques throughout his career as Victor's second hand man. Even though the prodigal son has betrayed those who trusted him the most, Owen has been impressed at how a young man like him can do so much at such a young age. Having a powerful father can only get a person so far without talent.

He is also fascinated with Amelia's poise and determination as the Legion's first lady. Although she has always stayed behind, he knows that she is critical to both Victor and Thom's success. Without a strong woman, neither of these men would have reached the level of greatness that they had. Victor would have given up on his men long ago and Thom probably would have never even joined the military without his mother. Having a reputation as a ladies' man, Thom was more interested in enjoying life than anything else. He would have been perfectly content wasting his parents' money.

As Iris continues to introduce the rest of the team, Amelia is getting more elated by the minute. She has not been this happy since the war began over six years ago. When she heard that Victor had died, she thought her world had ended. Now, she feels a burst of energy and a renewed sense of hope. This group of people seems to be on top of their game and she just cannot wait to start working with them.

Chapter 7: Drunken Stranger

After everyone has gotten comfortable with one another, it's time to have a plan. The first order of business is to come up with a name to call this group. Although they do like the name Legion, they cannot go around calling themselves that without arousing suspicion from everyone else. At the same time, they still felt they should honor Victor and his group. Ultimately, they have decided on the name La Rivincita.

It meant "revenge". The revenge that they would have on the Desiderios.

The second order of business for Amelia and her new band of fighters is to find Fouke. True, the one they *really* want is Thom, but that ship has sailed a long time ago. It's too bad, really. If they had him on the team, their success would most certainly be ensured. Without him, they will have to settle for the next best thing.

Even though not many people like the major personally, everyone knows that he has the connections and the military know-how that this young team needs. And, Amelia has the one thing that can sway someone like him – money, and lots of it. With this team of underground men and women, he is as good as found.

Within days, the La Rivincita has caught scent of Fouke. Iris has met an old man who claimed that he had been to Trozos Island after having one too many drinks at the local pub. He says that the island is beautiful place and he wished he was back there. If it wasn't because of his orders, he would jump on the next boat and sail there today. He then dares anyone who would go to have a drink with him. No one has accepted his challenge. In fact, most of the patrons simply look at him with disgust and move on.

Ordinarily, no one would have cared what a drunk has to say, but Iris is intrigued. For an impaired man who is just blabbering, it's too big of a tip to ignore. Very few people know about this island, let alone mention the name as if it were a paradise of some sort. Besides, no one who has ever been on that island has ever been seen alive on Balavan. How can a man like this have gone there and come back unscathed?

He looks like a regular man with nothing special about him. While he looks like he has a nice tan going, he does not look like an aborigine. Despite his slurs, he does not have a foreign accent. In addition, he does not look particularly strong or embattled. There are no visible signs of scars that would reasonably have been on a man who would have fought off cannibals. From the way he is drinking and carrying about, he look like a person from a civilized world with a few too many things on his mind rather than a barbarism that enjoys the taste of human flesh.

Waiting outside of the pub, Iris and Russell pretend to be on a date having a good old time laughing and drinking as they wait for the old drunk to stumble outside. By about 2AM, he finally emerges. Iris has never been so happy to see such a smelly and disorderly person. She is getting really tired of pretending to enjoy Russell's jokes and he in turn is getting bored of telling them. Immediately, they grab the old man and throw him in a car in the back of the alley.

Slapping his face a little, Iris says, "Hey, wake up."

The old man looks at her with bloodshot eyes and slurs something that sounds like, "Hey, you are sooo pretty" before passing out in the back seat.

Russell laughs as he says, "well, that was expected," before patting him down.

Rolling her eyes, Iris puts a blind fold on the old man says, "Haha, very funny. He's our man. I am sure of it."

The only thing Russell finds in the old man's pockets is some loose change and a key. There is no form of identification, papers, weapons, or anything useful on him at all.

"What exactly do you think he is the man of?" Russell continues as he drives off.

"For starters, he seems to know a lot about Trozos Island that contradicts popular belief."

"So? He's drunk. He might have just been making things up."

"Even if that is the case, I want to know why he chooses to make up that story or what the rest of it is."

"What does his story have to do with *him*?" Russell says trying to avoid saying any names in case the old man is faking his drunken stupor. There is no telling if he is an agent sent by the Desiderios to infiltrate the new rebels.

"Everything. It's the closest island. Remember. Even though he was last seen going East instead of West where the island is, he was seen on a small boat. Considering the size of the vessel, it's unlikely that he went anywhere far."

"If you think he is on Trozos, why bother to talk to this man? Why not just send someone there now?"

"It's just a hunch. Besides, if the island is filled with cannibals, I would rather that we are a little bit more prepared. If it's not, we don't want to barge in on the islanders fully armed. Anything he can tell us about the place is better than going in blind."

Soon, they reach an empty building that is still being repaired. Going to one of the finished rooms with the old man over his shoulder, Russell drops him on the floor and says, "Watch this one. We will be back in the morning."

"Yes, sir," the guard says.

There are a guard in two corners of the room and one in front of the door. They are all wearing military fatigue with a ski mask covering everything except for their eyes and mouth.

As they leave, Russell takes out the key and asks, "What do you think this opens?"

Iris looks at it and says, "That looks like an ordinary key that opens the door to his house."

"I guess you are right, but aren't you just a little curious?"

"Oh, come one! We are neither children nor burglars. What can you possibly want to find in his home?"

"I don't know. When you first picked him up, I didn't think much of him, but now that I have thought it over, I do think he is a person of "interest," as he puts his hands up to make quotation marks in the air.

"Even if you want to snoop in his house, you have no clue where he lives."

"For now, but I am sure I can find out," Russell says as he smiles.

"What do you think you can possibly find there? Considering that he has nothing on him, he is either very careful or very useless. Either way, it's not worth the trouble."

"Maybe. Maybe not. If he does not have the discipline to stay sober enough not to blab in a bar, I would say he is *not* a very careful man. Besides, even if he is careful, I am sure one of us can find the dirt if there is any to be found. Considering what he seems to know, I highly doubt he is useless. That is such a strong word." Russell says confidently.

"OK, I apologize. I should not call him useless, but not very helpful to our cause. How about that? Is that good enough for you?" Iris responds sarcastically.

"Better!" Russell says with a grin.

He almost never wins an argument or discussion with her. It's a moment that he wants to savor for a little bit longer. They were steadily heading to a hardware store. Taking the key to a machine, he makes a copy before handing it back to her.

"Here, if it makes you feel any better, you can return the key to him before he wakes up."

*

As morning comes, the old man blinks his eyes, but he cannot seem to see anything. The room is simply too bright. His throbbing headache doesn't help either.

Handing over a glass, the guard says, "Here, drink this."

The old man looks at him with squinting eyes. For a split second, there is fear in his eyes, but soon it dissipated.

"Do you mind telling me where I am, sir?" the old man asks as he tries to adjust to the light.

The guard does not say a word.

Sniffing the water, the old man says, "Is this water?"

"Yes,"

Laughing, the old man says, "This isn't laced with poison or anything, right?"

"No," the guard replies seriously.

Looking at the water for another second, the old man says, "Bottoms up!" as he chucks down the whole glass.

Then, the old man asks, "Am I in trouble?"

Once again, the guard is mum.

"Can you tell me anything?"

He gets the same response. Taking a sigh, the old man sits on the floor and says, "I guess I am a prisoner."

Looking at the two guards and the room, the old man knows that he is in an interrogation room. Three sides are simply white walls and the fourth side is a mirror. Iris and Russell are on the opposite side of the mirror studying their latest source.

"He must have done this before since he is way too calm for someone who has just been kidnapped," Russell says.

Nodding, "Mmm, he's definitely a pro. Are you ready?" Iris asks.

They both put the ski masks and both look just like the other male guards. Iris's cloth is intentionally baggy to conceal the fact that she is a woman. She has also learned how to walk like a man. Along with her voice alternator, it is difficult for anyone to guess otherwise despite her short and petit frame.

"Good morning," Russell starts the interrogation. "How did you sleep last night?"

"Very well, thanks for asking," the old man replies.

Iris is impressed that the old man remains so poised. From her experience, most of people she kidnaps are usually a little bit more rattled than that. Even if they appear to be in control, she can usually sense a heightened level of adrenalin in the form of increased breathing, faster heart beats that show through the chest, or higher pitched and faster speech. She cannot sense any of them here.

He appears to be right at home. There is no sign of the drunken man from the night before, which raises a definite alarm. She has a feeling in her gut that she and Russell have been setup. The good thing is they have prepared for such a possibility, which explains why they are holding him in the middle of nowhere.

Nevertheless, she wonders whether or not meant to be kidnapped. If so, who is he really? Who does he work for? Judging from his age, he looks like a very experienced pro, which does not faze Iris much. Despite her young age, she has taken down men who are very skilled.

Pretending that everything is as it should, Iris says, "Why don't you start by telling us your name?"

"You can call me John. What do I call you?" the old man replies with a grin.

Obviously, that is not his real name. It's too generic to be of any use, but Iris decides to ignore it for now.

"OK, *John*. You can call me Mary and call him Jim. What do you know of Trozos Island?"

"Haha, good one!" the old man says with a laughter.

He knows very well that neither side is willing to give up their real names, but that's ok – at least for now.

Continuing to play the game, he says, "Isn't Trozos Island just a land filled with cannibals?"

"Uh, huh. Then, do you mind telling me why you said you want to be back there last night."

Laughing, the old man replies, "Is that what I said? I sometimes drink a little more than I can handle. I have no idea why I would have said something like that."

Sensing that this conversation is going nowhere, Russell changes the topic and asks, "Where do you live?"

"On the other side of town."

"Oh, great, this man is filled with vague answers," Russell thinks to himself as he bites the corner of his lip.

Then, Iris asks, "Why did you seek us out?"

Laughing, the old man says, "Ah, so you figured it out!"

"Do you know who we are?" Russell asks with a very serious tone.

"Yes."

"Who are we?"

"You are the people looking for Major Brandon Fouke."

"And what makes you think we are looking for this man?"

"For starters, I heard you last night."

"So, he was faking it!" Iris says to herself. This old man is not nearly the fool that he pretends to be. On the other hand, he may be a very useful ally.

Playing dumb, Russell says, "I didn't mention this Major Fouke last night. Just answer the question, old man. What do you want from us?"

"It depends. Do you want to find him or not?"

It's interesting how the old man has turned the tables on these two. They normally have the upper hand. This is the first time that the person being interrogated becomes the one doing the interrogating, but Russell is not about to let that happen. From what he has already heard, he knows that the old man has the information that they need without giving a straight answer.

Russell ignores him and says, "Who do you work for?"

"Don't worry. I do not work for the Desiderios, if that is what you are asking."

Fair enough, both of them know that there are certain things that they would never divulge to an ally as long as they answer enough to be on the same side. If either one of them was in the same situation as the old man, they would have given a similar response.

"Why would you want to help us?" Iris continues.

"I am helping you so you can help me."

Another excellent answer. Nobody ever does anything out of the goodness of their heart, at least no one Iris has ever met. If he is telling the truth, she won't have to speculate as to what exactly does he want from them.

"How do you expect us to help you?"

"I don't want Fouke on my island as much as you want him here."

Ah, so he *is* an islander and Fouke is not as welcome as he thinks he is. After having taken off for the last few weeks, he must have overstayed his welcome, but doesn't know it yet.

"Your island? You just said the island is filled with cannibals. If you don't want him on your island, why don't you just eat him?" Russell says sarcastically.

"Yes, we could, but we don't want to."

"Why not?"

"All I can tell you is that I have my orders."

"Fair enough. Before we get down to business, we need to get some things out of the way first." Russell says as he stares into the old man's eyes. "First, we need to do something about our trust level. I don't think either one of us has a warm fuzzy feeling about the other yet. How do you propose we fix that?"

Grinning, the old man extends his hand and says, "Hi, my name is Torgny. I am from Trozos Island. I was sent here by Chief Cai."

"Well, that's a good start," Russell says.

"Your turn," Torgny says.

Both Russell and Iris take off their masks. Not wanting to speak for his sister, Russell simply says, "I am Russell."

After a brief second, Torgny looks at Iris as she removes her voice activator. "Hi, I am Iris."

Smiling, Torgny says, "It's nice to meet you both, finally."

Iris is amused that he is not surprised at all that she is a woman. He is also not bothered by the fact that they have not offered up any information besides their face and first names. It's as if there is no need for them to tell him because he already knows.

Just to be sure, Russell asks, "What do you know about us, Torgny?"

"I know that you finally showed your faces to your benefactor."

Laughing, Russell says, "Are you saying that *you* are our benefactor?"

"Oh, no, my good man. I am talking about the awe inspiring Mrs. Richardson, of course."

"How do you know that?" Iris asks in amazement.

"You may be good, but you are still young. All that driving around doesn't fool anyone. But, I have to admit. The look on Mrs. Richardson was *priceless!*" Torgny replies as he laughs heartily and wipes the corner of his eyes.

Feeling a little embarrassed, Russell asks, "Where were you?"

"Around. I have been following Mrs. Richardson for a long time now."

Upon hearing this statement, Iris is very concerned. She is wondering how long this stranger has been watching them without their knowledge. Even though he has only admitted to following Amelia, she is sure that he is doing the same with them considering that Amelia is helping them. How much does he really know? And, most importantly, how does he plan on using the information that he has gathered?

Obviously, once a spy learns something valuable, he always relays it to his superior. Hence, it's safe to say that his Chief Cai knows about their operation, which can be a major problem going forward.

Looking grim, Iris asks, "Yet, she has never noticed you. What is your mission exactly?"

"Like I said, I am here to try to get Fouke home and the poor widow is about the only one I can think of who may want him back badly enough to get it done fast."

"Why haven't you approached her yourself?"

"My mission is to remain anonymous. Mrs. Richardson should never know that I am involved."

"Then, why reveal yourself to us?"

"After watching you, I figure you want secrecy as much as I do. Am I right?"

He knows he is, but wants some form of acknowledgement.

After a moment of silence, Torgny asks, "So, do we have a deal?"

Nodding, the three of them shake hands. After giving them a few instructions on how to enter Trozos Island without being captured, they part ways.

As the old man leaves the room, he nods to the guard, grins, and says, "See you later. Keep up the good work."

While the guard is somewhat put off by the strange gesture from a drunk, no less, he keeps his composure as he greets his two superiors farewell.

*

Within hours, Russell and two of his men are prepped and on their way to Trozos Island. Boarding a sailboat, they dress like average sailors from Balavan. There is no hint of military anywhere on them. As instructed, they do not carry any menacing looking weapons. They do, however, bear presents – big, beautiful ones that can be easily seen from shore. Most importantly, they raise a flag that Torgny has given them. It is green with a white anemone in the middle, which is unusual but at the same time not all that strange considering that they are sailing through the ocean.

Thinking about the flag, Russell is actually a little embarrassed, because he had missed it when he searched the drunk the night before. It was sewn into his inside pocket. Because it was well folded, he did not even realize there is something in there, but begs the question – what else did he miss? He didn't hear any rustling of paper during the pat down, but there may very well have been.

As they approach, he is getting an eerie feeling. A question keeps coming up in the back of his mind. Is Torgny setting them up? After their conversation, it's obvious that this seemingly drunken old man is much smarter and more experienced than he is. There is no telling what they will step into when they land.

Yet, at the same time, he seems so trustworthy. He doesn't know why. It's just a gut feeling. It's like the one he had when he first learned the identity of his father. For years, his mother did an excellent job of hiding the truth from him by telling him that his father had died a long time ago. Hence, when David Carson finally found him when he was a teenager and told him that he was his son, he did not want to believe him, but he did. Maybe, it was the fact that they have the same eyes or the way he spoke.

In this case, there is no physical evidence that would lead Russell to believe him, but he *wants* to. Besides, he cannot think of a reason for Torgny to lie. Knowing Fouke the way he does, he is probably being the same selfish man trying to take advantage of the islanders. Even if he hides it, his true nature eventually will show itself.

Chapter 8: Failed Rescue

As soon as they can make out the shore, people start flocking to the beach looking at the strangers in the boat while some of the children are pointing at them. Seeing the crowd of families, Russell is excited. Come on, what kind of monster would kill visitors in front of their wives and children, right? Then, he sees the skulls and the skeletons spread across the shore line, reminding him that this is a well-known group of cannibals. Even though Torgny looks civilized enough, he wonders if he set him up to get eaten. At that moment, he visibly shakes as a chill comes down his spine.

Taking a deep breath, he says, "Alright, men, be sure to keep calm and look friendly."

While his men nod their heads, they know that he is saying it as much for himself as it is for them. As soon as they arrive, there are about a hundred people waiting for him whispering. Then, the crowd parts and a group of men in two rows come marching towards them.

Then, the two rows part ways showing an old man and a young woman. From the way they look, Russell already knows that this is Chief Cai and his daughter. Taking a leap of faith, he decides start off the discussion by giving his real name.

"Good afternoon, your majesty. My name is Russell Angleton. We are very humbled by your presence," he says as he takes a deep bow.

Whispering something to his daughter, Chief Cai pretends not to hear or understand him. Meanwhile, Nimue plays her part and simply nods.

Clearing his throat, Russell motions to his men who proceeds to take the gifts out of the boat and says, "We come bearing gifts. I hope it's to your liking."

The two men slowly take the treasure box off of the boat and carefully walk towards the chief. Before they reach him, however, one of the men on the side steps in and blocks them. Knowing that's their cue to stop, they put down the box and slowly open up the chest to reveal the precious items that Amelia has given them. As one guard quickly searches through them to make sure that there is nothing dangerous in the box, the guards bring the chest closer for the chief to inspect.

While the contents are not priceless gems or gold, they are exquisite items such as silk robes and fine art. Considering that they are humble soldiers, Chief Cai is actually quite impressed with their offerings even though he does not show it. By the fact that the chief is not insulted, however, Russell at least knows that he is still on the right track.

After a minute, the two men bow as low as Russell did and start to back up without turning their backs on the chief. Watching his men, Russell is glad that he has chosen these two. Being in such a hurry to capture Fouke, it has slipped his mind to tell them before they landed. From where he is standing, he has nothing to worry. They have the proper etiquette for greeting a king.

As soon as he Russell congratulates himself, however, he instantly knows that it is not going to last. Then, chief gets up, shouts something in his native language and everyone hushes. Even the babies have stopped their fussing and the dogs have stopped their barking.

The only sound he can hear is the ocean lapping at the shore and the sea gulls up ahead. Not sure what to expect, Russell and his men do not move a muscle. As they await the chief's next move, they feel as if they are frozen in time.

Without realizing it, all three of them have stopped breathing at that moment.

Like when Fouke first arrived on the island, Chief Cai says something to his daughter and she proceeds to translate it.

"Welcome," she says.

Only at that moment do the three men take a deep breath again. Russell says, "Thank you, your majesty."

"What brings you to my humble island?" the Chief asks through Nimue.

It's a simple question, but is not as easy to answer as it appears. First, he does not want to discuss Fouke in front of the entire village that has come out to view the spectacle. If he does, there is no way Fouke is going to just hang around and wait for them to catch him.

Second, he does not want to tell the whole village that he has met Torgny. Knowing that secrecy is of the utmost important thing to a spy, broadcasting that he has met one is not a wise thing to do. Of course, by bearing the flag that Torgny has given him, it should be obvious that he must have gotten it from someone from the island. After all, it is quite unique and not one that can be easily forged.

After careful thinking, he merely says, "I have come to seek the advice of your majesty."

Intrigued, Chief Cai has never heard anyone make that request before. Usually, he hears some lame excuse like the one that Fouke gave him.

"What is it you want to know?" the Chief asks through his daughter.

"I apologize, but it is a matter that I must discuss in private."

The Chief whispers something to his daughter again as she nods. Russell is trying to read either one of their faces to see if he can gauge whether or not he is going to be in hot water, but they both seem to have a poker face. From their eyes and mouth to their hands and breath, there is not a single twitch to give away their mood.

Then, the daughter says, "Come with us."

Relieved, Russell takes another deep bow and says, "Thank you, your majesty."

As they follow the king and the princess, the two rows of armed guards walk closely behind them. Before today, he has never felt a situation like this before. When he was a part of the original Legionnaires, he was a mere trainee who was so insignificant that no one ever bothered to shoot at him or surround him.

During the last few months, he has increased his status as a leader, but still remained behind the scenes to do strategies and tactically espionage. This is the first time he is actually in *enemy* territory. He doesn't know if he is exhilarated or terrified. All he knows is that his adrenaline is shooting through the roof.

*

Once they get to the chief's hut, the chief's guards block Russell's men. Then, they proceed to pat him down before allowing him to enter, all the while under the watchful eyes of two very large and mean looking guards. As the chief sits on his throne, he stares into Russell's eyes and begins talking.

With his daughter still translating, he says, "Now that I have indulged your request, you may speak."

"Thank you, your majesty. I apologize for inconveniencing your majesty, but I must have secrecy for

92

this conversation, not just for myself, but for a man whom I have befriended in Balavan."

Chief Cai knows what he is talking about. He stares at Russell again to see if he flinches. After he is satisfied with what he has seen, the chief says something in his native tongue and the two guards bow and exit the hut.

"Go on," the chief says through his daughter.

"I have had the pleasure of meeting Torgny."

The chief nods and motions for him to continue. After all, he already figures as much. The flag that Torgny has given Russell is not an official flag of Trozos. Instead, every spy has his or her own variation of the flag. While they may look similar, those who know about the system can tell whose it is just by examining it. By giving the flag to an outsider, it means that the person who has given the flag has already vetted him and has deemed him safe to enter. However, his spies usually deliver a report first before the outsider comes ashore. Without it, there is no way for the chief to know why he has sent the stranger to their home. For all he knows, this outsider may have killed Torgny and stolen the flag, even though, judging from his demeanor, it is highly unlikely.

"He has told me that a friend of ours may be on this island and we would like to bring him back with us."

Looking a little frustrated, the chief asks, "I thought you wanted to seek my advice?"

Being caught in his own little white lie, Russell is a little embarrassed. That is what he has said before being allowed to come into the chief's hut. He has to say something that will appease the chief before insulting him.

"Yes, I do," Russell says, "I need your advice on how I can bring him back safely."

"Is this some kind of a joke? You can take him any time. What kind of advice would you need?" the chief says as he starts to look a little angry.

It's obvious that the chief is not happy with what he has heard, even if it is just a white lie that gets him to listen. Panicking, Russell knows that he has to think of something quick again.

Remaining as calm as he possibly can on the outside, Russell says, "It's not as simple as that. He is a wanted man back home."

Although Russell knows that he is taking a risk by telling the truth, he feels that it is necessary. On one hand, he most certainly has angered the chief by confirming that a suspected criminal is hiding on his island. By admitting that he is his friend, it also makes him an accessory to whatever crime Fouke is guilty of. On the other hand, he can take this opportunity to vouch for Fouke's innocence and clear his name. If he can convince the chief that he is wrongfully accused, he may gain supporters on the island. As for the chief, even though he suspected as much, he has never heard anyone say that before.

Before the chief becomes enraged and demands that they all be thrown off the island or, worse, be killed, however, Russell says, "But, he is wrongfully accused and I need your advice on how I can help him return home safely."

This time, Russell has raised his voice a little. He has no idea who is listening in but he is not taking any chances. After scanning the area, he does not see Fouke, but that doesn't mean that he is not in earshot hiding somewhere. Knowing his reputation, it's always best to not say anything to anger the Major if he knows what's good for him. Fouke definitely remembers his enemies well and firmly believes in revenge.

The chief says, "Prove it."

"Alas, I do not have any hard evidence but I can tell you what I do know and hope that your majesty will believe me," Russell replies with sincerity.

"Humor me."

Russell begins to tell the chief about Fouke and the battle between the Legionnaires and the Desiderios. As soon as he mentioned Fouke's name, however, the chief is startled a little.

"That fake, lying bastard. I knew he was lying about his real identity," the chief mutters in his native language.

His daughter knows better than to translate that. She merely nods. After a short pause without hearing the princess, Russell continues his story hoping that he is just telling her something that is just between the two of them and has no relevance to him.

Like in any story, there are always two sides to it. As a member of the La Rivincita, he embellishes it to make the Desiderios sound like the bad guys. After all, they were technically the rebels even though they have every right to fight for themselves. That doesn't seem to matter to Russell right now. All he wants to do is to convince the chief to let him have Fouke. To lay it on thick, he makes sure that he describes how Fouke fought gallantly, but was forced to go into exile after his fellow men have been killed or captured.

"How are you related to him?"

"I worked under his command."

"So, you have personally watched his gallantry."

"Yes," Russell says with tongue in cheek, hoping that the chief didn't catch that.

"What do you plan on doing with him after you take him back home?"

"I plan on taking him to our hideout."

"Didn't he escape from Balavan on his own? What makes you think he will take the risk to return with you?"

"Unlike the day when he fled, we have built a following that is large enough to protect him now."

"How many people do you have?"

Russell is not comfortable telling the chief the details of his men. At this point, he has no idea which side the chief is on. Even though Torgny has made it sound like he is on their side, there is no telling if he is correct. Hence, he decides to throw out a large ballpark figure.

"We have over a thousand."

Sensing that he is lying, the chief decides to cross examine him and see if he fumbles.

"How many do the Desiderios have?"

Realizing that he has overestimated his own numbers, Russell is pondering how he should answer the question. Should he say that he has more or less than the enemy? If he says he has more, it may sound too farfetched to be believed. After all, it has only been several months, it doesn't seem all that reasonable to have gathered such so many men already. But, he has already given a definitive number and he cannot back out of it now without looking like he is lying, which he is. He really has no choice, then.

"They have about five thousand," Russell finally says.

Chief Cai already knows that Russell is bluffing. Even though Torgny has not given him a report about Russell, he has given him the lay of the land. He knows perfectly well what is going on. Based on the estimates that his best spy has given him, he knows that both numbers are wrong. At his best estimate, the Desiderios have at least double the number of men that Russell has given, which means that he probably only has a few hundred of his own, if even that.

Judging from his boyish looks, Chief Cai figures he has not been at his job for very long. For all he knows, he could be lying about his position or who he really is. He can be pretending to be the leader of the La Rivincita in order to kidnap or rescue this Fouke guy, depending on the angle he is playing. As long it's one or the other, Cai can care less which one. He has no affinity for the imposter who introduced himself as Gavin Anderson. He didn't really like him when he showed up and his daughter never trusted him. Now, he has confirmed that he is the infamous Fouke, he would be glad to get him off of his island, just like his trusting spy has said. On the other hand, Russell has to be telling the truth about *something*. Otherwise, Torgny would have been able to see through that and sent a warning. It would be interesting to see how it all unfolds.

"I will get back to you in the morning," the chief says as he waves his hand.

"Thank you, your majesty. I humbly await your word," Russell says as he calmly backs out of the hut.

As protocol dictates, the guards escort them to a hut that looks and feels like a small quaint hotel in an exotic vacation resort, complete with private guest rooms and a man who acts as a concierge. Yet, at the same time, Russell knows that it's also a form of house arrest. As he looks out of his window, he can clearly see that the guards are watching them from right outside of the hut.

*

As soon as he leaves, the chief turns to his daughter and says, "Can you believe this fool?"

Smiling, Nimue says, "He looks sincere."

97

"What? Are you kidding me, my child? He is lying through his teeth!"

"Yes, I know, he is, but he is doing it because he cares so much."

Slapping his own forehead, he says, "Please don't tell me you are actually letting your heart do the thinking for you – for once!"

Blushing, she waves her hands frantically and says, "Oh, no! You misunderstand, father! I merely mean that he is too young to perfect the art of lying. What I mean is that he seems to be sincere in his desire to help his friend, but does not know how to do it without getting himself in trouble."

Smiling, Chief Cai is amused by his daughter's embarrassment. He has been waiting for her to fall for a man for some time now and he senses that she has feelings for this rascal. Even though she is already 21 years old, she does not show any interest in any of the suitors who knock on her door, no matter how hard they have tried. By her age, her mother had already given birth to her, god rest her soul.

Not to make her any more uncomfortable than she already is, he changes the conversation and says, "What do you think of his proposal?"

Nimue is grateful that her father has not pressed any further.

Composing herself, she returns to her old self as the devil's advocate and says, "This Gavin or Fouke fellow sounds a little shadier than we originally thought. Even though he seems to be doing well living with Nonni and Grami, he may just be lying in waiting until the right moment to attack. If we don't get him off of this island fast, he will soon gain too much strength and we will no longer be able to defend ourselves against him."

"Hm, you have a point."

"Besides, now that we know someone else is looking for him on our island, we can no longer just kill him. This Russell fellow may have told other people where Fouke is. If he doesn't return with him soon, more may come and there is no telling what they are capable of. Even though they may have lost to the Desiderios, I hear that the Legionnaires were quite a formidable and ruthless bunch of cutthroats. I expect the new ones are not that different from the old. Even if they have lost their leader and many of their commanders, there are still some strong men amongst them."

Nodding, the chief says, "I agree. We certainly cannot let that happen. So, what do you think we should tell this Russell fellow?"

"I think you should hand our new friend Gavin to the boy."

Cai chuckles at her statement. He knows that she calls him a boy on purpose in order to degrade him. By making him sound like a child, she cannot possibly be interested in him that way.

Then, Nimue continues, "But we cannot just tell Russell where to get him. If he is telling the truth and that he is rescuing this man, no harm is done. However, if he is lying and is trying to capture him, this Gavin will try to run. So, we cannot risk tipping him off."

"Hm, another excellent point. How do you propose we get him to meet this Russell without telling him?"

"Easy. Just send out a royal decree. Gavin is not going to turn you down, at least not while he is still weak."

After a short pause, Chief Cai says, "OK. It's settled then. Please bring in the advisors as soon as possible."

"Certainly," Nimue says as she curtsies.

*

After telling his advisors about what transpired between Russell and himself, Chief Cai is waiting for their, well, advice. Like usual, he has to pry it out of them. There are simply too many indecisive people amongst his rank. He is glad that he already has his informal chat with his most trusted advisor, his daughter. He already knows what he plans on doing, but just wants confirmation from his counsel before making a decision that may impact the future of the village.

As usual, after a pause, he gets impatient and says, "Well?"

One man says, "I think we should get rid of all four of them. I don't trust any of them."

Another man says, "Hear, hear."

A third man says, "I thought Gavin, or whatever his name really is, is a nice man, but I am not so sure anymore. I cannot believe I let my children play with him! If he is Major Fouke, he probably killed a bunch of people before. Just thinking about having a man like that on our island just gives me the creeps. I say it's better to be safe than sorry."

Chief Cai has heard the cautionary words of this same man last time he asked about the same stranger. It's pretty obvious that the council members do not trust them. If he does not heed their words and something does happen to the island, he will never be able to forgive himself.

"OK, now that we have agreed to cast him out of our island, how do you think we should get rid of him?" the chief asks.

Then, the first man looks concerned and says, "I wasn't saying that we should cast them out when I suggested getting rid of them. I think we should kill them."

With those words, there is a string of gasps in the hut.

"Why?" the chief asks without looking surprised.

He has thought about the need to kill them, but he doesn't want to go to those extreme measures without a good reason. He is fully aware of the what-ifs. Yes, these men do seem dangerous and can pose a definite threat to everyone on the island, but they haven't *done* anything to show that they will.

The man replies, "We cannot take the chance. Looking at their history, the odds are against us."

"Yes, that may be true, but what happens if their friends come look for them?" the chief asks.

It's a legitimate question. Since they are part of an army, they are certainly not alone.

"We will kill them, too."

"Really? So, we are now in the business of killing rescuers?" the chief asks with a strong sense of sarcasm.

The council members all look in shock at this statement. Yes, they are used to the chief being sarcastic at times, but usually it's nothing more than that. This time, it looks as if he is dead serious. Upon hearing the remark, the man shuts his mouth and looks at the ground.

"I didn't think so," the chief says. "Anyone else?"

As everyone tries to avoid the chief's eye contact, one man stands out, as usual. It's Albin. He always loves to speak up during moment like this. It's as if he speaks only when he feels that it will make him stand out. Otherwise, there is no point joining in the discussion.

He says, "With all due respect, your majesty, if we do kill these men, how would their comrades know that? After searching them, they do not have any form of communication with them. Since the sea can be such a dangerous place, they can easily have been swallowed by the ocean. We can easily destroy their boats and scattered the debris close to Balavan and away from the island to throw them off of the scent. Then, we can decide whether or not we should execute these men."

Smiling, the chief knows that Albin has a good point. Meanwhile, after seeing the smile, Albin knows that he has done it again. He prides himself in saying just the right thing without wasting his breath. Looking at Nimue, however, he is not quite as satisfied by her expression. She is merely leaning against the pole like she always does. She doesn't look the least bit impressed with what he has said.

As expected, he turns to her and says, "What do you think, princess?"

Looking at him coldly, she says, "What I think doesn't matter right now. You should be more concerned with what the chief thinks."

Laughing, the chief loves these little banters. It's like a lover's quarrel, but not quite, since they are not lovers.

"What does everyone else think?" the chief asks.

The heads begin to nod again.

"So, it has been decided," Chief Cai says. Turning to Albin, he points at him and says, "I want you to destroy their boats and scatter the debris as proposed." Then, turning towards an advisor who has been silent during the entire meeting, he asks, "I want to get to know these newcomers a little bit better. Got any suggestions?"

Being put on the spot, the man stutters for a second without saying a single intelligible word.

"Never mind," the chief says before turning to another advisor and asks, "What about you?"

Even though he is also taken by surprise, he at least has a few extra seconds to prepare after watching the first man sweat. Despite knowing that it's not the best answer, it's the only thing he can think of at the moment.

"How about we invite him to a feast tonight?"

"Ah, a man who likes to party," the chief replies with a smile.

Encouraged by the chief's casual comment, he continues, "And get them drunk. A man who drinks too much has loose lips."

"Spoken like a man with experience!" the chief says with a hearty laugh.

The man doesn't know whether or not to laugh with the chief, but decides to do so politely anyways. After all, he is not sure if the chief means that he personally talked too much after being drunk or that he has experience eavesdropping on others who have been drinking. In either case, neither one of them sounds flattering.

"Anyone else? Or does everyone think that we should be wining and dining our potential enemies?"

"What about Gavin?" Nimue asks.

"What about him?" the chief replies.

"A public feast will definitely tip him off that his rescuers are here. When they arrived, Nonni and Grami did a great job of keeping him busy inside their house as they are instructed, but a party makes way too much noise for him to ignore."

"True. That means we have two choices. We can either interrogate them or hold a private dinner with just us and the guards."

"I have no problem interrogating the Russell fellow. He looks like a pleasant enough of a man. I can get him to spill under the right circumstances. But his two goons look like the kinds who are more into fighting it out than talking it out. Putting them in a holding cell may not have quite the effect that we want."

Looking that the man who suggested it, the chief says, "Hm, go ahead and arrange a small dinner party, then. Nimue, if you can be so kind as to keep our guests busy while we do this without arousing their suspicion."

As the princess nods, the chief looks at everyone else with disgust and says, "The rest of you are dismissed."

Chapter 9: Special Treatment

While the chief and his council are discussing the fate of the newcomers, Russell is pacing back and forth in his room. He is not sure what he should do. Should he sneak out and try to look for Fouke on his own? It would be too dangerous. He doesn't know anything about this island and has no idea where to look. Even though the chief seems like a reasonable man and Torgny is definitely sophisticated, way more than their reputation would make them out to be, it doesn't mean that the rest of the islanders are just as cordial. Who knows? There may be people who actually practice cannibalism in the backwoods somewhere.

Besides, he risks betraying the chief's trust, which is something he is not prepared to do yet – at least not yet. After the chief indulged him by allowing him to have a private audience, he should keep his end of the bargain and just wait for the chief's word like he has agreed to do as a gentleman. Of course, if he is forced to betray the chief, however, it will have to be a last resort. Russell has always been the kind to use his brains more than his brawns to resolve any issues. This is no different. As he gets more restless with each minute, he hears a knock on the door. What can it be? He doesn't know anyone on this island.

"Has the chief made his decision already?" he ponders.

As he quickly goes to open the door, his anxiety decreases. It's the two men who came to the island with him. The tall and muscular one is Cameron, the translator who was recruited into the original Legionnaires alongside Russell. He is well versed in the language of the Trozos. Hence, he knows very well what the chief is saying without the help of the princess. Because of his massive physique, he is often mistaken as a bouncer; however, he is nothing but a gentle giant. He hates violence, which is an odd trait for a military man. He really only joined the Legionnaires so he can have a chance to travel and experience some adventure. Because he is fiercely loyal, however, he comes in very handy for Russell.

The second man who came along for the ride is Owen, Russell's half-brother. Although he is tall and thin, he is actually stronger than he looks. As a school teacher, he is also not the fighting type. Instead, he likes to help around the school, building things for the children to play with or learn from. He was quite terrified to be on this mission, but he was more than willing to do it. He joined the military because he heard that his half-brother and half-sister are both in it and he wants to be able to work with both of them. Well, he got his wish. He gets to watch over his baby brother and have his back.

"Hey, fellows. Come on in and make yourself comfortable," he says as they walk in.

"What now?" Cameron asks.

"There is really not much we can do right now," Russell replies grimly.

"Nonsense! We can explore and learn about this island and see how much or, rather how little, of what we know about it is true," Owen says naively.

"I respect your enthusiasm, but don't you think it's a little reckless? We are not exactly on a sightseeing tour here," Russell replies, sounding more like the no nonsense older brother than a younger one.

"Well, excuse me! I thought we are trying to make the best of it," Owen replies, sounding a little hurt.

"I am sorry. I didn't mean to snap at you. It's just that there is a lot at stake here and I am just a little rattled. That's all," Russell says.

Sitting at the table, Cameron is quiet, but cannot believe what he is hearing.

"How can two grown men be so sensitive at a time like this? Shouldn't they be more worried about whether or not the cannibals will eat them than their feelings? Whatever, it's their call. Guess that's what happens when you have two brothers on the same team," Cameron says to himself.

Turning to Cameron, Russell says, "You have been quiet. What do you think?"

"What do I think about what?"

"Do you think we should explore or stay here?"

Cameron knows a loaded question when he hears one. He knows very well that he is only asking to make his brother feels better. By asking a third person, he is pretending that what Owen says is worth considering when he has already shot it down previously.

"I can go either way. If you want to explore, I am for it. After all, we are burning precious daylight. As a member of La Rivincita, I think we can fend off whatever danger may come our way," Cameron says while Owen smiles.

Right when Owen thinks that he has won this round, however, Cameron finishes his thought.

"On the other hand, it may be easier to extract Fouke if we follow the chief's orders. The less trouble we create for him, the faster we get what we want," Cameron finishes his though ever so politically.

As the three continue pondering their next move, they hear a knock on the door. Its only 3 in the afternoon. The chief cannot possibly have come back with an answer so quickly. Being the cautious one, Owen reaches for his gun on his holster before realizing that he didn't bring it, under specific instructions that Torgny has given them. Looking at the other two, Russell nods at them, which is a signal that they should spread out in the room to minimize being attacked at the same time and be on their guard. Then, he answers the door slowly hoping that he is not going to be killed on the spot.

As it opens, Nimue is standing there in a beautiful tribal dress complete with flowers adorning her hair, her wrists, and her tiny little waste. She also added extra makeup, giving her such a bright glow that Russell cannot take his eyes off of her as he is mesmerized by her beauty.

Taking a bow, the princess smiles and says, "I hope you gentlemen are comfortable here."

After realizing that his mouth is open, Russell composes himself and says, "Yes, of course, princess." Clearing his throat, he says, "What can I do for you?"

"Nothing at all, my good sir. On the contrary, I am here to make sure that you are comfortable. It would be so rude of us to not show our hospitality."

Snapping her fingers, Nimue signals for the ladies to come into the room. As they start walking in, all three men cannot believe their eyes. Each is beautiful and exotic. While some are bearing food ranging from fresh fruits to steamed lobsters, others are bringing tools like palm leaf fans and jars of sweet scented cream. At that moment, Russell pinches himself. This cannot be real. Has he died and gone to heaven? He has been to parlors, spas, and burlesque shows back home, but never in his life has he seen so many gorgeous women in one room. As an added bonus, they are all here to make *him* comfortable!

Even the ever stoic Cameron doesn't seem to be immune to the effects that these lovely ladies have on them. He is also in awe as he stands there watching them set up their stations and laying out their equipment. In the middle of the room is a table with no less than 30 dishes on the table. Next to it is an inviting lounge chair lined with soft wool of lamb. Three of the ladies are busy putting different items on three plates, getting ready to feed it to their guests.

By the left wall, a couple of ladies have set up an impromptu massage table. Even though it is made out of wood, it is covered with a blend of leaves and flowers that look and smell wonderful. There are also bottles of different massage oil at their disposal. On the right side is a tub that the ladies are filling with hot water as one of them pours in several varieties of aromatic oil. While each smell delicious, the combined scent is indescribably divine. After about 20 minutes, the ladies all stand in attention next to their stations to signal that they are ready.

Then, Nimue smiles and announces, "What will be first, gentlemen?"

The three men look at one another, not knowing what to say or which to choose.

After a long silence, the princess says, "Don't worry. You will have plenty of time to enjoy all of them. Perhaps, you would like for me to choose for you?"

With that, the ladies spread out and grab a man towards their station as they giggle like little school girls. The men are now putty in their hands. They have completely forgotten their missions or where they are, just the way Nimue likes it.

"Please let me know if we can be of more service," the princess says as she quietly leaves the room.

Of course, the men are already so hypnotized by the ladies surrounding them that they can no longer hear anything. As the ladies take off the men's shoes to put them in their respective chairs, they are completely unaware of their surroundings. Even if there is a war breaking outside of their room, they probably would not have noticed. After a few minutes with no response, Nimue cannot believe how easily these men can be distracted as she walks away. Why wait for a stuffy dinner party? She can get these men to talk way easier her way.

*

On the other side of the island, Fouke is acting as if he is going about his business as usual, but he is not as dense as he pretends to be. Despite Nonni and Grami's best efforts to keep him away from the news, he has caught wind of the two strangers who have come bearing gifts. It's not hard really. Without an official decree from the chief to keep it quiet, word spreads like wildfire. In all reality, with the number of witnesses, there really isn't much that the chief can do. Even if he commands it, somebody will have a loose lip. Just about everyone on the street is talking about them. While the adults chitchat with one another, the children are having little make believe games pretending to be Russell and his men. Before long, Fouke is well aware of the three strangers.

The truth of the matter is by showing up in some a grandiose manner; Russell is hoping that Fouke will hear about their landing. It makes his job that much easier. Even though the island is not large, it can be dangerous and difficult to find a person, especially when he does not want to be found. By saying that he is here on a rescue mission, Russell is hoping that Fouke will reveal himself first.

Being a skeptical man, however, Fouke is not about to take his word for it. Even though Russell worked for the Legionnaires before their humiliating defeat, the Major has no idea who this man is. After all, he was merely a new trainee towards the end of the war. It would have been nearly impossible for Fouke to have met him amidst all of that chaos. At the time, he was more preoccupied by the impending doom and his own safety than anything else.

One of the main reasons that Fouke has survived for so long is because he has learned early on to never trust anyone before vetting them first. He usually does it in the background rather than face his target one on one. With his title and reputation, most people immediately put up a front when they first meet him, which completely defeats the purpose. He wants to see them when they do their normal daily routines to see if they are honest and loyal or secretive and scheming. He usually does not have a problem with people who are conniving as long as they do their job well.

There is no point asking Nonni and Grami for information. He already knows that their job is to watch over him. The only time they ever talk to him is when they ask him to do things for him. It can be anything from tending to the herb garden and gutting a fish to repairing a wobbly table or shoveling manure out of the stables. All he is going to get are more chores. In order to get a little more information on the strangers, Fouke decides to offer his help to one of his more gossiping neighbors.

Knocking on her door, he says, "Hello, there! Is anybody home?"

He knows she is because he heard her laughing loudly not more than five minutes ago, but he asks anyways in order to look the part of an innocent nobody.

Coming to the door, the lady says, "Oh, hello, Gavin. How are you?"

"Good, is there anything I can help you with today? I have some free time and I am in the mood to help out a lovely lady," Fouke says as he forces as genuine of a smile as he possibly can.

"Oh, you are such a darling!" the lady says as she drags him inside her hut. Then, she says, "I don't have anything that needs to be fixed, but how would you like to have lunch with me and the ladies?"

Inside her kitchen are five older women sitting around the table, sipping tea. All of the ladies stop their conversation to greet him warmly. Two of them even get up to give him a hug before pulling up another chair for him. While those in Balavan may be shocked by their display of affection for this self-serving coward, those on the island are used to it. After all, he has offered each of them his help more than once before. Each time, he has done a wonderful job and has been a perfect gentleman. Over the last few months, he has been doing one backbreaking task after another, winning the hearts of the locals.

"Is there anything you ladies need?" Fouke asks politely.

"Oh, look at you! Such a dashing young man!" one of the older ladies says.

Even though Fouke is well into his 30's, he is still young, at least compared to her.

The lady of the hut says, "Come on, ladies! Why don't we cook him a nice big meal to thank him for all of the work that he has done for us?"

Like a bunch of schoolgirls trying to impress the football quarterback, they are start giggling and talking amongst themselves, trying to figure out who is going to make what for their special little man. To them, he is like a little golden boy who can do no wrong. From the exterior, Fouke is sitting them with a polite smile on his face. Inside, he is getting a little impatient. He doesn't have the time to wait for a hearty meal. Knowing how long these ladies take to do anything, it's going to be two hours or so before they are done in the kitchen.

He doesn't have that kind of time to waste. If Russell and his men are here to capture him, he needs to know that now so he can plan his escape strategy. Even if they are here to rescue him, he needs to know as much about them as he possibly can so he knows how best to manipulate them. He

112

simply hates having to fly by the seat of his pants. It gets him all rattled and frustrated. When he is like that, there is no telling what he may end up doing. Besides, if he stays too long, Nonni and Grami will get suspicious and come look for him. By then, it will definitely be too late. If they find out that he is looking for information, they may lock him down and watch him even closer than they have been.

Walking towards the group of ladies, Fouke says with a grin, "Perhaps, I can help here, too? I am not just a man's man, you know. I wouldn't mind trying my hands in the kitchen if you ladies will teach me."

The ladies all laugh at his comment. It seems everything he says is funny to them, just the way he planned. From his experience on the island, sweet talking old ladies is the fastest way to get anything from gossip to new clothes – free of charge.

"Of course, darling!" one lady says.

While one of the ladies shows him how to knead the dough for the pasta and cake, another is trying to show him how to braise the turkey. After a few minutes of buttering them up, he figures it's time to milk them for information.

"So, I hear that three men landed on our shores this morning," Fouke says as he looks at everyone with a boyish grin.

Even though Nonni and Grami have told the ladies not to tell him anything outside of pure gossip or idle chatting when he first came to the island, they completely ignore her words. After looking at his angelic face, they cannot imagine that he can be anyone sinister.

After a second, one of the ladies says, "I hear they are from Balavan."

Pretending not to know anything, he looks surprised and says, "Really? That's where I am from! What are the odds?"

"Oh, that's right! No kidding. Small world!"

"What do you think they are doing here?"

"We don't really know, but we have heard the rumors," one of the ladies says with a wink.

Ordinarily, Fouke would have shuddered at the gesture, but he keeps it to himself. He knows that it's important to keep playing his role.

Another lady chimes in and says, "We have heard that they are here to rescue *somebody* important. Hint, hint."

Looking confused, he asks, "I don't get it. Who are you ladies talking about?"

Giggling again, one of the ladies puts her finger on her mouth and whispers, "Shhhh, I hear they are here for *you*!"

"For me? Whatever for?"

"Oh, my sweet little man. I think it's all a load of baloney. Rumor has it you are some hotshot military man. Are you?"

"Who? Me? What? Are you kidding?" Fouke says as he blushes and laughs.

"I didn't think so. I have no idea where the rumor comes from, but I also hear that this man he is looking for is a ruthless cutthroat. Can you imagine that? A cutthroat in our very island! I would rather die!" one of the ladies says as her eyes get bigger.

"Wow, he does sound scary. Do you know what his name is?" Fouke says innocently.

"Oh, I don't remember," one of the ladies says as she looks at the others.

"I think it's something that starts with an F, like Farm or Fork, or something like that."

Laughing inside, Fouke finds it hilarious and sad at the same time that they think he is a farm or a fork. It's amazing what people will make up.

"I think it's Fouke," a third lady says.

"Oh, yes, that's it. Do you know him, dear?"

"Fouke? Hm, I think I have heard of him," Fouke says as he looks like he is thinking.

"What kind of man is he?"

"I don't really know him. I just heard of him. Nothing much really. Just that he is a Major in the Legionnaires."

"So, why do you think he has such a bad reputation?"

"I don't really know," Fouke replies, trying to get them to stop asking about him. Instead, he wants to redirect them to Russell and his men. "What about the three men who claim to be here for him? What are their names?"

"The main guy is called Russell something, but I have no idea who the other two men are. From what I heard, they didn't introduce themselves."

"Yes, I don't think they are that important. I think they are just his bodyguards or something."

"Bodyguards?" Fouke laughs to himself. Even though he has never met Russell, he is wondering how in the world a snot nosed new recruit like Russell can get bodyguards so quickly. Even he didn't get one until after many years of service. This kid must be someone special. Fouke is regretting that he didn't take any personnel files with him when he escaped – not that he had the time or cared less about anyone else at the time.

"So, did they have any luck finding this Fouke?" Fouke asks.

"I doubt it. If they found him, everyone would certainly be talking about it."

"I wonder what they are doing now," Fouke asks lightheartedly.

"Oh, I heard that the princess is treating them like honored guests!" one lady exclaims as she claps her hands.

"Really? What is she giving him?" another lady asks.

Leaning closer, she says, "I hear she has gathered two dozen of her ladies to give them the full treatment, complete with the finest food, massages, and whatever else they ask."

"Wow! That does sound wonderful."

Then, a fourth lady asks, "I wonder who this Russell really is to get that kind of special treatment. I cannot remember the last time that the princess has gone all out for someone like that before."

The fifth lady says, "That's because she never has. Usually, her ladies only cater to her and no one else."

"Maybe he is the general in disguise!" one of them says.

"Oh, he would be such a dashing young general in uniform, don't you think!" another lady says as the rest of them continue to giggle at the thought.

"Oh, he better not be!" Fouke thinks to himself skeptically.

He is glad that the ladies have brought it up, even if they are simply joking. Nevertheless, they do have a valid point. He must be someone very special. For someone his age that didn't exactly stand out when he was in the Legionnaires only a few short months ago, circumstances must have changed in his favor. In other words, Russell must have learned something very important or has gained a special secret connection with someone powerful. In either case, it translates to bad news for Fouke.

If Russell is as commanding as Fouke fears, that can only mean he works for the Desiderios now, which is going to be devastating for him. He must consider this important and potentially deadly scenario. It is entirely possible that this Russell has switched allegiances and is using his previous connection to the Legionnaires to trick him into going back with him. Russell will probably use his boyish charm and innocent looks to lure him, but he is definitely not going to fall for any of that.

As Fouke contemplates on the best way to avoid being captured by this charlatan, one of ladies turns her attention back to him and says, "But, of course, he couldn't be as dashing as you, darling!"

"Oh, of course not! Nobody can be as handsome as our little Gavin!" the ladies tease.

Fouke has heard enough. He is not about to waste another minute sitting around when Russell is here to capture him.

After pretending to be embarrassed by the old ladies' teasing, he suddenly looks surprised and says, "Ladies, I apologize. I am having such a great time that I forgot that I have to go. Nonni is expecting me back any minute."

"Oh, so soon? But we haven't finish cooking your meal yet!" the ladies protest.

"Oh, I really want to see how the meal turns out. I hope I did everything right!" Fouke says humbly as he discretely looks out of the hut to be sure that this Russell and his thugs have not found him yet.

"Of course, dear! How can you possibly mess anything up?" one of the ladies says.

Laughing inside, Fouke is amused at how clueless they are. At the same time, he is very proud of the new persona he has created. Based on their sincere behavior, he is the apple of their eyes. It's as if they have taken him in as their adopted son.

Not wanting to delay any further, Fouke bows as he looks at every one of them in the eyes as he says, "Thank you so much for your hospitality, ladies, but I truly must go. We should do this again when we have more time."

Then, he quickly leaves the hut and goes towards Nonni's house as the ladies wave good bye to him.

The lady of the hut says, "I will bring some over later!"

Knowing that they are still watching, he turns back and replies, "Thank you!" as he begins to run.

*

Instead going in to Nonni's house, however, he goes to the back of the house to pretend to tend to the gardens. Once out of sight, he heads straight into the palm trees in the back. After looking around to make sure that he is not being followed or watched, he takes the hand-held shovel from the herb garden and starts to dig behind a large rock. Within minutes, he stops. Inside is a wooden chest that one of the other ladies in the village gave him as thank you for helping her clear her garden. It's not fancy, but quite roomy and sturdy with several layers and pockets.

Opening the chest, it's obvious that he has been collecting his loot for some time. There are several different types of weapons in it, ranging from a small dagger to a long sword that spans the length of the trunk. There are also arrows and bows as well as poison darts. The only thing missing that he would have loved to have in there is a gun. Oh, how he misses his prized pistol. He couldn't carry it with him on his journey because he knows that the islanders would certainly have taken it away from him as soon as they see it. In addition, having a weapon like that around aborigines only invites suspicion, which is something that he definitely wants to avoid when he is alone.

Inside his treasure trove are various tools ranging from a compass and binoculars to ropes and nails. Some of these things he had brought with him from Balavan, but was confiscated when he was arrested and given to the villagers as a part of his goodwill for being on the island. It took him great lengths to get them back. Short of stealing them back, he has tried just about everything from sweet talking the new owners to scaring them with lies.

For example, he told one old woman that a compass shows her where the devil is and if she uses it too often, the devil will know where she is and come for her. He almost feels sorry for her when he saw how absolutely terrified she was to hear the story. She practically begged him to take it back. He is quite surprised at how superstitious some of these islanders are.

In addition to the gadgets, he also stashes several different sets of outfits as well as items such as rouge and wigs for camouflaging purposes. In times of danger, he is not above dressing like a woman if his life depends on it. In fact, he has done that in the past before. Being a thin man, he actually looks pretty good in women's clothes if he takes the time to do it right. Underneath all of that is a bright shiny object, which looks like a mirror, but is much more than that. It is actually hiding a secret compartment underneath where he hides all of the jewels that he has received for helping out the islanders. While everyone on the island thinks that he is doing all of these odd jobs for free, he is actually making quite a tidy sum of money doing them.

Taking out a dagger and a few poison darts, he carefully puts them on his belt. He also takes out his binoculars and puts on a large but plain coat to cover it all.

"Now, let's see who this Russell *really* is," Fouke mutters to himself as his eyes turn back to his sinister look.

Chapter 10: Violet's Big Break

Looking out of the window of her office, Violet is glad that everything looks perfect just the way it is. Balavan has been rebuilt and has returned to its former glory. Traces of destruction and death are virtually wiped out. Cars are everywhere as people return to their normal hustling and bustling routines. Streets are clean. Stores are aplenty. Children are playing in local parks. Adults are going to back to work.

Yet, she knows that her work is nowhere near done. While Fouke is trying to figure out what Russell's angle is on Trozos Island, Violet continues to search for the elusive man back home.

It's been months since she started the search and she is getting more discouraged each day. A part of her is sure that he has left the dominion. If he was gone for good, she couldn't be happier, but she knows that is too good to be true. Knowing him as well as she does, he is bound to come back for what he thinks he deserves. After looking high and low from back allies to exquisite hotels, it seems the trail has gotten cold, very cold. When the war first ended, there were thousands of possible sightings every day. Now, the Desiderios are getting about one every two weeks. Violet knows that she needs to change her strategy. With each passing day, she fears that he is building a new army and planning to take back Balavan by force.

Feeling depleted, she figures it's time for her to take a walk around town to clear her head. Despite being 28 years old, she still looks quite youthful, which is amazing considering what she has gone through up to this point of her life. With teenage blemish years well behind her, she has flawless skin with full and luscious hair. Dressed like an average upbeat high school student, complete with smoky eye shadow, artistically manicured nails, and bright layered clothing, she easily blends in with the other teenagers.

As she walks aimlessly for a few minutes, she sees a coffee shop and decides to go in and take a break. She can definitely use a nice cup of coffee for a quick pick-me-up right now. As she waits for her latte by the counter, she looks around the shop. Everyone seems so alert with the caffeine flowing through their veins. There are teenage girls who are laughing and talking about 200 words per minute over one another. There is a woman typing quickly on her phone without stopping and a man talking on his phone in a very heated tone. It's obvious that some of them need to go to decaf before they bust a blood vessel.

Then, she sees a familiar face. It's Amelia. Unlike the last time she saw her, Amelia is not dressed in her usual fancy outfits. There is no hat, no oversized lace and gold trimmed purse. Her jewelries are understated. She is not even wearing her giant wedding ring, which she has continued to wear even after she thought her husband has died. Instead, she is wearing a simple but tasteful gold band on her ring finger with barely any makeup on her face. Her outfit looks like she bought it off of the rack rather than from the latest designer that she is known to wear. It's obvious that she is trying to blend in, kind of like Violet herself.

"What in the world is she doing in a coffee shop so far away from her home?" Violet wonders.

She is much calmer than most of the other patrons as she casually sips from her cup and reads a newspaper. Judging from the weathered and bent pages, however, it looks like a very old issue. Upon closer inspection, Violet realizes that it is from the day that Victor lost the war. After all of this time, she is still going over the same article over and over again.

Can't blame her, really. From all accounts, she was a very devoted wife who loved her husband very much. She would hold on to him for as long as possible.

Feeling sorry for the widow, Violet cannot imagine what Amelia must have been going through during these past few months. Staring into Amelia's face, she sees definite signs of aging even though she is still quite beautiful. The loss of her husband must have been hard on her. Thom's betrayal can only make it worse. She hopes that she never has to face the same fate as she.

Yet, at the same time, Violet sees a determined look on the old woman's face. Violet wonders if Amelia is actually reading the article or plotting his vengeance when she reads it repeatedly. She is pretty sure that Amelia has memorized every word of it by now.

"Why does she look so serious?" Violet ponders.

Then, she knows the answer as her eyes brighten. Amelia must be trying to get her revenge. After giving her home to Thom, Amelia seemed to have retreated to the country place more or less willingly. Because she has never taken an interest in politics, Violet has discounted her as a possible threat. Now, she is not so sure. Looking around the shop to see if someone else is here with Amelia, she does not see anyone in particular.

"She cannot be here alone, can she?" Violet wonders.

Scanning outside, she does not see the car that Victor favored nor any other fancy cars parked outside. There also does not seem to be any bodyguards watching over her or chauffeur waiting for her. From the looks of things, she has either given up or no longer cares about her status or life style. It she has, it's for the best. The elder Richardsons were always too full of themselves anyways. It's time for them to come down a notch and join the rest of the world. Of course, she knows better. She still has her intelligence team watch over her. After all, the Richardsons have never been the kind to just take it and admit defeat. They would have never reached the status they held if they did.

As she continues to look around the room, she notices another interesting individual. He is also an older individual. Like Amelia, he is sipping his coffee slowly as he reads a newspaper, but his is new and crisp. Unlike her, he looks like he is reading current events rather than reminiscing the past, like a normal person would. Occasionally, he puts the paper down and writes on it. It appears that he is filling out a crossword puzzle of some sort. It seems only the older folk care for the old fashion newspapers while all of the younger patrons are all on one form of electronics or another as they nervously go about their business.

There is nothing that stands out about him. He looks like any other man. He is dressed in a collar buttoned down shirt and black slacks and loafers. There are no odd pieces of jewelry, not even a wedding ring. He basically looks like any old man and does not give out a hint of suspicious in any way. Perhaps, that is a clue in itself, trying to look *too* normal if there is such a thing. That is certainly her goal.

As she continues to study him, however, she realizes that she has been made. He is looking at her the same way she is looking at him. Now that their eyes meet, he picks up his hand and waves at her as he smiles. Even though he is a pleasant looking man, she feels a little uncomfortable for having met his eyes. After all, she has never seen him before. Her initial reaction is to shudder.

"Why is that old geezer smiling at me?" Violet laments.

She is used to people hitting on her, but usually not from someone *that* old. Then, she realizes that perhaps it's her fault for looking in his direction in the first place.

"Oh, wait, maybe he is just being friendly," Violet says to herself blushing a little.

After all, he has not gotten up to introduce himself. In fact, he has directed his attention back to his paper. Just then, she eats her words. He folds his paper back up and starts to walk up towards her.

"Oh, oh," Violet says to herself as she turns back to the counter to focus on her coffee.

"Excuse me, miss," the old man says as he stands right behind her.

Lifting her head up slowly, Violet fakes a smile sheepishly and says, "Yes?"

"Would you happen to know what time it is?"

"OK, that is a lame pickup line if I ever heard one," Violet thinks to herself.

She cannot believe that she has screwed up and attracted his attention. Out of thirty people in this shop, he has to ask *her* what time it is. It's kind of embarrassing for a high school girl to be hit on by an old man like that in front of all of these people. Any other girl would have walked out on him. As she contemplates on doing the same, she stops herself as she realizes why he has targeted her. This is no coincidence or a cheesy attempt at hitting on a woman more than half his age. In the corner of her eye, she sees Amelia getting up at the same time and leaving the shop. He must be her distraction. Nevertheless, she is not about to let him know that she is on to him.

Looking at her watch, she says, "It's half past ten."

"Thank you, miss," the old man says as he exits the shop.

Then, it dawns on her that the newspaper that he has been writing on is gone. Amelia must have taken it with her. Now, it's clear. Whatever he has written is not a puzzle. It is a message to her. She must find out what. And, she is curious as to who this old man is. She has never seen him before. He is almost as old as Victor. As soon as she walks out of the shop, however, he is leaning against the wall waiting for her.

"Hello, again," he says.

Surprised, she replies, "Hello."

"Are you looking for me?" he asks with a grin.

Looking a little upset, she says, "What in the world makes you think that I am looking for you?"

"Oh, I don't know. It must be my boyish charm," the old man says as he starts to laugh.

"What do you want?" Violet asks bluntly.

"It's not what I want. It's what I can do for you," he replies as he stares into her eyes.

"Ew, that just sounds *so* wrong," Violet says to herself as she quivers again.

Waving his hands, the old man laughs again and says, "Nothing of that sort, young lady! I don't know what you are thinking, but I am old enough to be your father!"

"You mean, grandfather," Violet mutters to herself.

"OK, my apologies. Grandfather," the old man says as he takes a bow.

Violet thought she was quiet enough, but apparently not. For an old man, he certainly has excellent hearing.

"All joking aside. I am here to offer you my help," the old man says. Then, extending his hand, he says, "It might help if I introduce myself first. My name is Torgny. It is lovely to meet your acquaintance."

"Torgny? What an unusual name," Violet thinks to herself.

She has not heard of this man from all of the intelligence reports that she has been gathering. She

126

wonders why his name has not popped up somewhere before since she is sure that he is much more than meets the eye.

Accepting his hand shake, Violet says, "I am Violet."

With that brief introduction, both sides seem to be a little more comfortable with the other. It seems that both are confident that the other has extended an olive branch by giving their *real* names without force. Yet, at the same time, Violet knows she cannot completely trust him because he seems to be quite secretive with his note passing earlier at the coffee shop.

"What exactly do you think you can help me with?" Violet asks.

"I don't think this is the best place for us to talk."

Snickering, Violet has seen this trick before. The man will pretend that he is going to help a seemingly weaker girl but has to talk in a quieter place. As the approach an alley or a parked car, a hand will go over the girl's mouth and she passes out. Next thing she knows, she wakes up a victim of kidnapping or worse.

"I don't think so. You are going to tell me what I want to know here," Violet says as she shakes her head.

"I see you need a little convincing," Torgny says with a friendly smile.

Violet has also heard that one before. It's a euphemism for: *he has a thug hiding somewhere who is going to beat her into submission.* Looking around, she checks to see if he has backup. Unlike inside the coffee shop, there is really nobody loitering outside or even standing still. The busy street is filled with people constantly moving. Looking at the adjacent buildings, there are no open windows either.

"Don't worry, Violet. I am not going to hurt you. I promise. I am a man of honor," he says, trying to convince her to at least listen to him.

"If you want me to trust you, why don't you start by telling me what you were writing on that newspaper back inside the coffee shop?" Violet asks calmly.

"Oh, that," Torgny says with a crooked smile. "That was a test."

"A test for whom?"

"You."

"Why?" Violet asks suspiciously.

"I wanted to be sure that you are the right woman to talk to."

"And?"

"I am talking to you now, am I not?"

"OK, smarty pants. Answer me this: why did Mrs. Richardson take your newspaper after you left it on the table?"

"Ah, see. You did pass the test. She took the newspaper because she doesn't trust me. She wants to see what I have written on it, just in case it's a secret code or something."

"What *did* you write?"

"I filled out the crossword puzzle. No doubt she is going to try to put the words together to try to see if she can find a clue," Torgny says as he laughs. "But she won't. It's just fun to mess with her sometimes."

"So, you have done this before."

"Oh, yes, many times."

"Then, why is she still falling for it?"

"Like I said, she doesn't trust me. She is convinced that one of these days I will actually leave something and she will regret it if she lets that slip through."

"Why do you torment a poor woman like that?" Violet asks.

"Poor woman? We *are* talking about the same Amelia Richardson, aren't we?"

"You don't think a woman who has lost her husband and has a son who betrayed her is poor?"

Laughing, Torgny says, "Well, if you put it that way, of course, but we all know that's not the whole story."

Violet is wondering what he means by that. He doesn't look like the cold hearted kind that can immediately discount someone else's feelings so readily. So, is he alluding to what Violet thinks he is? Does he know that Victor is still alive? Or, is he simply playing with the words and is referring to the fact that she is still a wealthy woman? No, that cannot be. He looks too intelligent and sophisticated for that. Regardless of his true meaning, she has to know this man better, but, like he said, not here.

"OK, you have convinced me. Let's go," Violet says as she starts walking.

*

Despite his frail and old exterior, Violet knows that this mysterious stranger is too dangerous to bring back to headquarters or any of the official hideouts. Even if he already knows their locations, she cannot risk showing him the inside or the entrances. There is no telling what he can do if he gets that close. Hence, she decides to take him towards the outskirts of town.

"Where are we going?"

"That's for me to decide and for you to find out."

Laughing again, Torgny thinks it's funny that she is such a firecracker despite dressing like a little high school girl. With these two, appearances are definitely deceiving. Violet is pretty certain that he knows a whole lot more than he is letting on, and she does not like it one bit. For starters, she is pretty sure he knows her real identity. For someone to talk to the Warrior that way, he must be either really stupid or really good. She is pretty sure he is not the former.

As they get within view of the river, Violet decides that it's far away enough from everyone else to start their conversation.

Stopping by a tree, she says, "OK, spill. What do you know about Amelia Richardson?"

"What do you want to know?"

"If you are going to answer a question with a question, I think we are done here."

"Oh, come on, I think that was a fair question," Torgny says casually trying to lighten the mood.

Unfortunately, it doesn't seem to be working.

"OK, everything. Is that a fair enough of an answer for you," Violet snaps.

Turning more serious, he says, "I apologize for upsetting you. I assure you that were not my intentions. I guess I will just start with the first thing that comes to mind. I don't want to bore you with information I am sure you already know, such as where she lives or what she does on a daily basis."

Intrigued that he knows what Amelia does every day, Violet asks, "What do you do for her?"

"Nothing," he replies.

"Then, how do you know what her routine is?" Violet asks impatiently.

Torgny is surprised by the question since he has not actually said anything yet. Instead, he quickly realizes that Violet does not know as much as she wants him to believe. With such an expansive intelligence group, he had thought that she must have known more, despite his hunch that she doesn't. In a way, he is glad. Now, he knows that she definitely needs his help. That also explains why she hasn't gotten anywhere yet with her desperate search for Fouke. Perhaps, the irony is that with so many people on her intelligence detail, she has gotten lost among the sea of information.

"I follow her," he admits.

"Why?" she asks dubiously.

Unfortunately, Violet is still clueless about what is happening. Ironically, she wonders if she is giving him too *much* credit. She is starting to think that he is nothing more than a peeping tom who is trying to profit from selling information to the highest bidder and she is the next victim that he plans on scamming.

"That's part of my job," he replies.

"Uh, huh, and what exactly have you found out?" she asks, trying to see if he is going to fish for some money next.

"Amelia stays at home most of the time, reading her husband's private journal. Once a week, she comes into town to get information from her special contact person. She prefers to meet either at busy places. The coffee shop and the little bistro on Main Street are her two favorites. She has also frequented the little antique shop on the other side of town."

Based on the information given, Violet suddenly realizes that this man is not the sleazy opportunist that she had thought. By giving just enough details to prove that he is telling the truth without giving away anything important, he is showing that he is quite the professional – extortionist or not. Being who she is, she figures she has nothing to lose as she presses to get more information from him.

"Why does she meet this person on a weekly basis?"

"Her contact gives her the weekly report on what is going on in Balavan. She also makes inquiries through this individual who gives her the answers the following week."

"What kind of inquiries?"

"Information on the Desiderios headquarter, for example," Torgny says with a mischievous grin knowing that it would pique her interest.

Then, a thought comes to her mind. Considering that Amelia took the newspaper from his table earlier at the coffee shop, can he be talking about himself?

"Are you her contact?" she asks directly.

Laughing, he says, "Oh, no, no. I am not a double agent. It would be against my principle to do that!"

"But you are not *my* agent, so, technically, playing Amelia on both sides may not be considered a double agent – depending on who you really work for."

Smiling, Torgny agrees with her statement, but whatever. There is no point arguing that point.

After a short awkward silence, Violet asks, "Who else do you follow?"

"You."

Violet is not happy with the answer, but is not really surprised as she asks flatly, "Why?"

"Because that is also a part of my job."

"OK, I get it. You are a spy who spies on everyone in the dominion."

"Well, not quite. I don't have that kind of time," Torgny replies as he shakes his head.

"I only follow those who are critical to my mission."

"And what is your mission?"

"Ah, the million dollar question," Torgny replies. After a short pause, he says, "My mission is to keep peace."

"Peace? What do you know about keeping peace in Balavan?" Violet asks sarcastically.

After all, she, as the head of the Desiderios, *is* the one in charge of keeping peace. If there is a higher authority working behind the scenes, she would definitely need to know that, regardless of how small or discreet they may be.

"I didn't say I keep peace for *Balavan*."

Ah, that makes more sense now.

"So, that makes you a spy," Violet says bluntly.

"Yes, pretty much."

"Then, why should I trust you? I should arrest you right now and shut you up."

"I am sure you can, but that might not be in your best interest."

"Uh, huh. If you don't tell me something that I want to hear in the next five seconds, I think I just might," Violet threatens.

While he knows that her threat is genuine, Torgny is not fazed by it in the least bit as he says, "Don't you care that I have just put two of your greatest enemies on my island? They are ready for you to destroy."

Startled, Violet is certainly not expecting that answer. Now, she is more certain than ever that this is a con man waiting to collect. Nobody does something like this out of the goodness of their heart. It's just too dangerous. He does not look like a man who is just out for a thrill.

"Which enemies are those?" Violet asks.

"Major Fouke and Russell Angleton."

At least, he got one name right. But, Russell Angleton? Violet is curious as to why he thinks this young man would be a threat to her. She has heard of him, but the reports she has gotten on him basically indicate that he is a tactician who works in the back as an analyst. While he is no doubt very intelligent, he is not trained for battles nor has been considered a leader by her officers. From what she knows about him, there is no indication that he may be a danger to the Desiderios.

"Should I elaborate?" Torgny asks rhetorically.

"Yes, please," Violet says as she nods even though she is expecting him to knock her up for some money before he says anything further.

Torgny begins by telling Violet that he works for Chief Cai of Trozos Island. She is surprised at first because, like everyone else, she has thought that the island is filled with cannibals. She would have never expected them to have such a sophisticated spy. Of course, that is just the beginning of the tale. After hearing that Fouke has been on his island for months, she is starting to get encouraged and enraged at the same time. While she is glad that she finally knows the location of the illusive criminal, she is angry at the face that her own men could not have told her that. By now, she is already convinced that he is telling the truth, but does not tell him that yet as she quietly and eagerly waits for more information.

Then, he switches the topic to Russell. First, he gives her a rundown on his earlier *drunken* encounter with Russell but leaving out Iris's name. Violet chuckles when she hears

134

that Russell fell for Torgny's act. Even though it doesn't change the fact that she herself also fell for his tricks, it makes her feel better about her own competence. He also tells her that Russell and two of his men have headed towards his homeland with the intention of capturing Fouke.

At the conclusion of his narration, Violet is literally speechless as she stares at him. At that moment, she has added two and two together. It is finally clear to her why Torgny thinks he is one of her greatest enemies. Being a former member of the Legionnaires, Russell must be trying to rescue Fouke and prepare him to lead a new rebellion as she has feared. At the same time, she cannot believe that so much has gone on without her knowing. If he is telling the truth, she needs to do something about her intelligence team. They are obviously too incompetent for the job. Perhaps, it was a mistake not to try to persuade Garret to stay on the team rather than take the job as the new sovereign.

Then, she simply says, "Thank you."

Torgny just smiles as he waits for her to finish her thought. He knows that it is a lot of information to absorb. Before he tells her what she should do next, like he did with Russell, he is going to give her the benefit of the doubt and let her figure it out first. After all, she is a seasoned leader, unlike Russell who needed a little push.

Then, she turns back to him and says, "So, what do you want from me?"

Laughing, Torgny asks, "What makes you think I want something from you?"

"Come on. What is it going to cost me?" she says as she gets straight to the point.

Looking a little hurt, he says, "I am actually a little insulted. I have not come to claim a reward. I am simply helping out a potential ally who needs a little hand."

"Why?"

"We have a common enemy."

By the look on her face, Torgny knows that he has said enough. It's time for Violet to sort it all out for herself.

Tipping his hat, he says, "We shall be in touch," as he turns back towards town and starts walking. Violet does not stop him. She knows that she will see him again if she has further questions. She is sure that he will show himself again no matter if she wants him to or not once she has sorted it all out.

*

Meanwhile, Violet has a million questions. First of all, while she knows that Fouke is evil enough for anyone to consider him an enemy, she wonders what Fouke has actually done to be called it on that ill-reputed island. Has he taken control of the island? That is not likely. He is not a risk taker. Regardless of his exterior persona, she knows he is a calculated coward than a brazen conqueror. If he had escaped there on his own, there is no way he would muster the energy to overpower a foreign government, especially one that he knows little to nothing about.

Then, what is it? What kind of hold does Fouke have on Trozos or its people? Is he secretly infiltrating the islanders so he can gain power? That is a much more likely scenario. Doing something secretive like that would be consistent with his sneaky ways. If he is, how does Torgny know about it? What kind of communication system does he use? Being an indigenous people out in the middle of the ocean, no one would expect them to have a satellite system or a cellular phone tower. Then again, maybe they do. If that is the case, perhaps, she can take advantage of it if she plays nice.

Wait a minute. What exactly is Torgny's plan anyways? Is it his plan all along to lure both the leaders of the New Legionnaires and the Desiderios onto the island? If so, why? Perhaps, he didn't send Russell out there just to get Fouke of his island, as he had told him. Instead, he sent him there to get Fouke out of hiding so the Desiderios can get him. Why else would he have told both teams to go after Fouke? But, the real question is why Torgny and the people of Trozos even care?

Knowing that she cannot solve the puzzle by herself, she decides to go back to headquarters.

Chapter 11: Decisions, Decisions

Being the leader of the Desiderios, Violet is not about to let this huge break slip through her fingers. Immediately, she calls her most trusted men to an emergency meeting. They are all surprised by the call. Since the war ended, they have not had a need to have impromptu sessions like this. As they start to arrive, they are all wondering what is going on.

While some are intrigued, others are excited. Have they caught Fouke? Is Violet retiring? Is Trip back? Or, are we about to be attacked? Has Thom changed sides?

As the men continue to speculate amongst themselves, Violet sits at the head of the table being solemn and completely silent.

"What gives? Now that Trip has taken a break, has Violet turned into him?" Sunny teases loudly at the table.

"No kidding! What happened to our bright and happy Warrior?" Clay asks.

Violet continues to remain silent until everyone has arrived.

"Good afternoon, gentleman. First of all, I know its lunch time. So I am going to start off by giving you my apologies for interrupting your meals. But, I have urgent news to discuss and it may take a while."

With that, everyone is quiet and turning towards her and giving her their undivided attention.

"I have just met an interesting man who has opened my eyes on what is going on under our very noses."

Concerned, Vick asks, "Who?"

"Interesting that *you* ask," Violet replies with a cold stare.

With Garret gone, the intelligence team is now being headed by Vick, one of the twin scouts who used to work for Garret. Even though they still argue with one another, he knows that he cannot do this massive job without help from his twin brother Valentine. Even though Vick is ultimately the one responsible for the entire operation, they share the duties equally. While Vick is in charge of the field agents who get the information, Valentine is oversees the group of analysts who try to sort them out.

Under his breath, Vick whispers, "Oh, oh," knowing that is not a good look from her.

She only stares like that when she is upset, which does not happen, especially not during peace time. And, he knows the anger is directed straight at him.

"What did I do?" Vick asks anxiously like a school boy who has been accused of doing something he is not supposed to.

He knows she has been concerned about Fouke from day one. Hence, he figures it has something to do with him, but from her uncharacteristic foul mood, it's not as simple as that. To avoid making her madder than she already is, he decides that it's better to keep his mouth shut for now and see what she has to say.

"It's what you didn't do," Violet replies angrily. Looking around the room, she continues, "Has anyone come across an old gentleman at the coffee shop or the bistro on Main Street lately? He is in his early 60's, medium built, tall, brown eyes, with salt and pepper hair and full beard?"

Confused, the men look at each other wondering who she is talking about. Her description is a little too generic to be of any use. There must be hundreds of men who fit that description on the streets every day. But, the fact that she points is out means that they are supposed to know who this man is. Each one of them is hoping that the person next to him does, because he has no clue.

Then, putting up a picture of Torgny that she secretly took at the coffee shop, she says, "How about now? Any ideas?"

The men still have no clue. It looks like a regular man drinking coffee.

"How about, has anyone come across anyone who may be following me around town regularly for the last few months?" Violet asks sarcastically.

That piques the men's interest as they turned from a confused haze to a concerned look. This sounds very serious. How can anyone not notice when a strange man follows their leader under their noses? Instantly, everyone looks at Vick and Valentine for an answer. Being put on the spot, the twins look at each other. Neither one of them has any idea who this man is.

"Since you obviously have no idea what I am talking about, let me tell you," Violet continues as she raises her voice just a little louder.

She proceeds to tell her team about her encounter with Torgny and everything that he has told her. Then, she pauses for dramatic effect as she stares at everyone's eyes, one after the other. It's as if she is an angry teacher looking at a class full of students who have failed a test. The room is so quiet that they can hear nothing but the humming sound of white noise.

"Well, what is your excuse?" she asks impatiently.

Vick stands up and says, "I have none, but to make amends I volunteer to go to Trozos Island to capture Fouke."

"That's great," Violet says sarcastically before asking, "And how do you plan on doing that with Russell and his men already there?"

Then, Thom says, "I will go with him."

Everyone is surprised that Thom has spoken. Ever since he betrayed his father, he has been keeping to himself, coming out only to do his duties of training others or for mandatory meetings. Other than that, he keeps to himself. He has not volunteered for anything since he became a member of the Desiderios. Then again, he has never really had to before. Because of the peace time, there really hasn't been anything that requires his skills. Being the former general of the Legionnaires, he is best at high level tasks such as strategies and tactics. Even before the betrayal, he often left the more humdrum tasks such as scouting or patrolling to the lower ranking personnel.

But, this mission is different. It's anything but mundane. More importantly, it gives him a chance to make a difference and perhaps redeem himself. Instead of the man who ratted out his father, he can be the hero who has finally brought down the last war criminal from those days. Besides, no one knows Fouke as well as he does. Because he was his former subordinate, Thom knows the subtle nuances of the disgraced Major better than anyone else, which is a very important quality considering that the man is such a chameleon.

Yet, at the same time, Violet is wondering whether or not Thom is ready for such an important mission. Is his emotional state strong enough to take it? Can he handle the pressure? The last thing she wants is for him to go there and completely break down, jeopardizing his own life as well as the team.

After all, as an elite member of the Desiderios, he knows a great deal of information that can be used against them. Looking at the determined look in his eyes, Violet thinks it's worth taking the chance.

After careful considering, Violet nods and says, "Yes, Thom should go on this mission."

Before Vick can open his mouth to protest, however, Violet looks at him and says, "But you will not."

"What? Why not?" Vick complains.

"Because you are supposed to be leading the intelligence team. Based on what I have just found out, you have a lot of work to do here."

As Vick leans back in his chair in frustration, Violet looks at him again and says, "It's critically important for you to find out which man amongst your team is a mole who has been sabotaging our efforts."

Surprised, Vick says, "What makes you think there is a mole in my group?"

"Can you think of another reason why you have failed to find anything useful after going after the same man for so many months?"

Stuttering, Vick has nothing to say.

Violet continues, "It's either that or you are admitting you are completely incompetent."

There is a uniform gasp in the room. No one has ever heard Violet talk that way before. She is *really* angry. Even though they do not like this side of her, they know she is right.

"Who else wants to volunteer to go with Thom?" Violet asks.

Seeing that his twin brother has egg on his face, Valentine tries to redeem his family name and says, "I will."

Nodding, Violet figures that Thom can use a good scout on his team. Thom has never been to a place like Trozos

142

before. Having a silver spoon in his mouth his entire life, he has never been face to face with a savage before and cannibals certainly counts as one. He will need Valentine to make sure that he doesn't fall into their traps. Although Vick is still a little hurt by his own rejection, he is confident that his brother can succeed in his place.

"Who else?"

"I will," Wolfe says.

This must be a special mission. It seems another quiet team member volunteers for this dangerous assignment so uncharacteristically. Being the animal specialist, he prefers wild beasts over men any day. Perhaps, it's the promise of the untamed wilderness that intrigues him. After months of peace time with humans, Wolfe is dying to see something more primitive. An island full of cannibals seems to fit the bill.

"OK, it's set, then. The three of you go recruit some men to go with you. The rest of you are dismissed, except you, Vick."

*

After everyone else clears the room, Vick says, "OK, first of all, I apologize for screwing up. I know it's my entire fault. I should be more vigilant and figure out that there may be a spy in my team before hearing it from you. I am really, really sorry."

"I am not here for your apology," Violet says bluntly. "I want to apologize if that is what you think I am looking for. What I am really concerned about is that our operation may be compromised."

Taking a sigh of relief, Vick is glad that he is not in the doghouse.

143

Seeing his misguided sense of happiness, Violet says, "Don't get me wrong. I am still mad at you. If you had done your job properly, we wouldn't be having this discussion."

Looking sheepish, Vick cannot believe how short his brief moment of celebration is.

"I need you to find this Torgny fellow and find out everything you can. I have to warn you. He is highly trained and he can sniff out a fake or a trap easily. He can either be our greatest ally or our greatest enemy. You must be very careful not to get on the wrong side."

Nodding, Vick says, "Understood."

As he gets ready to leave the room, he laughs and says, "I thought you were going to lecture me about the mole, not to give me an assignment."

Violet responds, "You are. I have a feeling Torgny knows who your spy is."

"By the way, I am assuming you want me to find him at the coffee shop," Vick says rhetorically.

"Don't worry. As soon as he gets wind that you are looking for him, I am sure he will turn up."

Vick is not sure if he should be scared of this man or not as he nods again.

Before Vick gets very far from headquarters, he knows that he is being followed. Expecting to see Torgny, he turns around to greet him, but he doesn't see anyone. Vick looks all around him, up in the buildings, inside cars driving by, inside shops along the street – nothing. Impressed, Vick continues to walk towards the coffee shop, sure that the mysterious stranger will show up there on cue as he enters the store. Alas, he is going to be disappointed.

After sipping his coffee for about half an hour, there is still not Torgny. He is disappointed that the elusive man hasn't revealed himself. He is wondering if the fact that he knows exactly what the stranger looks like may have dissuaded him from revealing himself. After all, secrecy is a vital part of any intelligence officer. If he is as shrewd as Violet says, he must know that she took his picture. Just as is about to give up and reaches into his shirt pocket to get his wallet and pay the tip, he feels a piece of paper in there. Surprised, he takes it out and reads it.

It says, "Meet me by the river bank at 5PM."

Looking around, he cannot believe that this man put a piece a paper in his shirt. He is really embarrassed now. How does the head of the intelligence team not know when someone reaches into his pocket? It is practically the oldest trick in the book! This is more than humiliating. It's mortifying. Yet, as hard as he can think, he does not remember anyone bumping him as he was making his way to the coffee shop.

Looking at his watch, he has about 12 minutes and the river is 15 minutes away. He has no time to waste. He rushes to the river as quickly as he can.

When he gets there, he looks around to see if he can spot the old man, but, again, he is nowhere to be seen. Vick is starting to get upset. This stranger is just playing him again! He has no time for this little game. As he is about to leave in a huff, he sees an old homeless man sitting on a bench. Reaching into his pocket, he takes out whatever loose change that he has and gives it to the man.

"Thank you, kind sir," the homeless man says with a grin.

"Not a problem," Vick says as he keeps walking.

Then, all of a sudden, he stops and realizes that the homeless man looks eerily familiar. Is that Torgny? As he quickly turns around, the old man has disappeared.

"OK, he is definitely testing me now," Vick says to himself.

Sitting back down on the same bench, Vick shouts, "Come on, don't you think this is a little childish?"

Several people stop in their tracks and look in his direction. He looks around to see if any of them may resemble Torgny, but doesn't see any immediate candidate. Then, the passersby mumble to one another before going about their own business.

"Well, at least I look like a crazy person now," Vick says to himself.

Then, he hears an old man laugh. He looks up and, finally, it's Torgny.

"What took you so long?" Vick asks with a stern voice.

"I don't know what you are talking about. I was here promptly at 5 o'clock just like I said I would."

"You were that homeless man weren't you?"

"What do you think?"

"So, why the game? What do you want from me?"

"I want to show you how easy it is for someone like Fouke to elude your men."

Somewhat insulted, Vick is not happy with what he has heard, but he knows that Torgny is certainly right. He has stumped him so many times already in such a short time period. First, he sneaks in a piece of paper undetected. Then, he posed as a homeless man. Now, he just appears seemingly out of nowhere even though he is looking around for him.

"Fair enough, but answer me this. Why are you showing me my failures?" Vick asks bluntly.

"If I am going to help your men capture Fouke, you need to do something about your training. Do you know how many times your men have been in the same room as Fouke and not seen him?"

"So, he is going to drive the dagger into my back when I am already down. OK, I deserve it," Vick tells himself.

"And where am I going to get this training? Are you offering your assistance?" Vick asks.

"Give the man a cigar, he gets it!" Torgny replies sarcastically as he pats him on the shoulder.

"How much is this going to cost me?"

"What is it with you Desiderios? Everyone is assuming that I am doing this for money," Torgny says as he refers to Violet's earlier offer.

"Because it's the most obvious reason."

"It's sad when everyone thinks that a person cannot do something simply out of the goodness of one's heart."

"Are you?"

Laughing, Torgny says, "OK, you got me there. No, but the fact that you were willing to give money to me earlier when you thought I was a homeless man is encouraging. At least *you* are not totally selfish."

"Don't put too much stock in it. It's just an instinct."

"Ah, but a good one."

Waving his hand, Vick says, "Don't change the subject. Tell me what it is you want in exchange for training us?"

"I want to be a part of your team," Torgny replies bluntly.

"What? Are you serious?" Vick says skeptically.

"Don't get me wrong. I have no intention of defecting or anything. I just think that we can be allies."

"Who? Trozos and Balavan?"

Although that sounds like a sarcastic question, it isn't, at least not to Vick. Even though he is not as good of an intelligence officer as he can be, he knows enough.

For starters, he knows that Chief Cai is extremely protective of his island and wants as few people on it, or even to know about it, as possible. There is absolutely no reason for him to want to make an alliance with anyone from the outside. Besides, if the rumors that it's a cannibalistic culture are anywhere close to the truth, there is no way that the chief of such a backward island would care about diplomacy. Hence, there is no reason why these two groups may want to join forces as a whole.

On the other hand, he wonders if Torgny has a personal reason to join the Desiderios without the consent of his superior. Perhaps, he has been on Balavan too long. Is it possible that he is now more in tune with Balavan's culture than his homeland? After all, there is no trace of a brutish cannibal in him at all. In fact, he looks quite sophisticated and civilized. Considering his politeness, some may even say that he is more so than most of the locals. He even sounds like one of them.

"Who else?" Torgny asks rhetorically.

"Why?"

He really wants to know how Torgny plans on answering this question.

"The stronger our neighbor is, the fewer problems we get."

"But, wouldn't an alliance require that Trozos be open to outsiders?"

"Not necessarily."

"You mean you want a secret alliance, one which even the people of either land know nothing about."

"Exactly."

"How do I know that you are sincere?"

"I am handing you both Fouke and Angleton. How else do you want me to prove it?"

"How do I know that it's not a trap?"

"You people don't trust others much, do you?" Torgny says as he shakes his head.

"Would you?"

Laughing, Torgny says, "I don't blame you. You don't really know me even though I know you. Well, the offer is on the table. Just let me know soon. The offer does have an expiration date."

After Vick nods to acknowledge the old man's offer, Torgny take off quickly. Even though he questions the old man, he knows that he *should* believe in him.

So far Torgny has bent over backwards for the Desiderios without really asking for much in return. Yet, no matter how many times the old man explains it; there is a nagging feeling in the back of his mind that there is more to it than he admits. Like the old adage says, if it's too good to be true, it probably is. What is he *really* after?

Even if it is a trap, Violet is only sending a few men over to Trozos Island. Yes, the men going over there are pretty important members of the team and they would definitely be missed if something were to happen to them. On the other hand, even if the islanders do kill everyone once they arrive, the damage to the Desiderios, or Balavan for that matter, is not all that great. It may be cold to admit it, but the dominion will go on. It's not like Violet or Trip is going.

"Wait, is that it?" Vick is turning over in his head. "Is Torgny trying to separate Violet from the rest of the team so he can target her?"

This thought is quite troubling to him. Now that Trip is out of town. Violet is the only one who can lead them.

Scratch that. Violet has always been their true leader. While Trip is awesome in his own way, she is the one who can inspire the team. The Desiderios would fall apart without her. That much is certain. But, then again, everyone who knows anything about the Warrior fears her. She can take anyone out even if she is taken by surprise. Missing a few members of the elite team is not going to change that. Besides, there is no way Torgny knows who are being sent to Trozos. Is there?

On the other hand, he can certainly guess. If he knows the Desiderios as well as he thinks he does, he would have guessed that Violet would not have sent him and that Thom would be more than willing to get a chance like this to redeem himself. So, is this an attempt on Thom's life? Even though they are not exactly friends, he cannot let a fellow member of his team walk into his death. This is beginning to sound like the most possible scenario. After all, just about every former member of the Legionnaires hates Thom, especially Fouke. Is Fouke behind all of this? Instead of sending this Russell fellow to capture Fouke, is he sending him as reinforcement?

He needs to get to the bottom of this as quickly as possible. Another old adage comes to mind: keep your enemies closer. Perhaps, Torgny wants to help train the intelligence team so he can find out their secrets and destroy them from within on this end while Fouke and Russell get their revenge on their side. No thanks.

*

After coming to the dismal conclusion, Vick hurries back to Violet to tell her what he thinks is going on. As she listens, she is more and more convinced that he is making a compelling point. Although she is still frustrated with the

150

problems in his division, she is glad that she has chosen him to head the department. Being a former scout, he has that special sixth sense that others do not possess. The only problem is that talent seems to only kick in when they are in danger.

Hence, there are two sides to this revelation. On one hand, this may explain why he is not aware of the mole in his own organization. While the mole has prevented them to be effective, he or she does not pose any imminent danger. The only harm being done appears to be slowing them down and wasting their time. Over the last few months, there haven't been any reports of attack. While Violet knows very well that there are still some disgruntled members of the old Legionnaires, they are but a shadow of their former selves. Without a leader, that is all they will ever be. If this Russell person is to be their leader, there is nothing to worry about considering that he is nothing but a bookworm.

On the other hand, it can mean that this Torgny is the imminent danger that the Desiderios may be facing. Being a treacherous man who is too smart for his own good, he has proven to be quite stealthy and manipulative. While this is a great asset for his employer, it spells bad news for his intended target. In this case, that would be the Desiderios. While her initial reaction is to get rid of him, she knows that he can be a very valuable resource. He is indeed one of those rare enemies who is better alive than dead. She needs to bring him to her side before he does something so devastating that she cannot undo the damage. But, how can she do that without jeopardizing their operation? After pondering her options for a few minutes, she finally decides that she has to take the chance.

"I want you to accept his offer." Violet says.

"What? Are you serious?" Vick says with wide eyes.

"Yes. Needless to say, you must make sure that he does not compromise us in any way, shape, or form."

"And how do I do that? If he is to train my team, he will know exactly what we are doing. It's a catch 22. There is no way around it. Even if we don't tell him explicitly and try to hide it from him, he will know exactly what we are planning, because he will be the one who taught us to do it. We are essentially inviting him into the deepest part of our lair."

"Relax. Don't be so paranoid. You have to have a little faith, sometimes," Violet says as she tries to cheer him up.

"Really? You really think we should do it?" Vick says, not sure what to think.

"Of course, we are not going to just leave him along. We are going to keep him in surveillance the entire time. And, we are going to let him know that we are watching him."

"Don't you think that's going to jeopardize my team's relationship with him?"

"Not at all. He is going to expect it. But, telling it to him up front, at least he knows that we are being honest about it. I am hoping that this way he will learn to trust us, too, and not just see us as a pawn to his real plans."

"Of course, that means you will need to get to know him on a personal basis. And, I mean *really* know him. I want to know everything there is to know about him. What his favorite food is? Who his past relationships are? Where does he hang out? Where was he trained? Even what his favorite color is? And, I don't mean for you to straight out ask him, if you know what I mean. "

"Yes, yes, I do."

"We need to stay on top of things. Knowledge is the key."

"Understood," Vick says before leaving.

Meanwhile, Thom, Valentine, and Wolfe have gathered a team of thirty men and are ready for their trip. Unlike Russell who carried nothing but gifts with only two other men to accompany him on his humble little boat, this crew is packing heavy. Carrying cannons and heavy artillery on their fortified boat, they are prepared for a fight without any attempt to disguise themselves.

Why would they? They are proud soldiers of the Desiderios who are on a mission to capture a well-known criminal. Unbeknownst to the Desiderios, Torgny has not prepped them the way he did with Russell. He never bothered to give this group a flag or any specific instructions. It's just as well. They probably wouldn't have heeded his advice anyways, considering that they are seasoned veterans, unlike Russell.

Chapter 12: Heaven on Earth

Back on Trozos, Russell and his two men are in heaven. Nimue's ladies are doing a wonderful job of keeping them preoccupied. They are completely unaware of the danger that they are facing from both Fouke and the Desiderios. For the moment, they have totally forgotten the fact that they are even on a mission. So far, they have proven that they are not experienced enough for such a mission. While the princess is making the final preparations for the private party, Russell and his men are like putty in the ladies' hands after having drunk glass after glass of their finest wines. As instructed, the ladies have taken the opportunity to insert some questioning while during the pampering sessions.

"So, how do you know where we are?" one lady asks.

Russell replies, "Oh, this old man back home told us."

"Who?"

"What was his name again? Tori? Courtney? Oh, that's right. Torgny," he replies as he slurs a little.

"How did you meet him?"

"Oh, I am an elite member of the La Rivincita. Don't you know? My sister and I caught him in a bar when he was drunk," Russell brags.

The ladies find it ironic that Russell is talking about capturing a drunk while he is under the influence himself.

"Who is your sister?"

"Iris. She is awesome!"

"What a pretty name! What does she do?"

"She can do anything. I wish I can be as cool as she is, but I am not," Russell announces loudly.

Russell then tells the ladies everything about Iris's connection with Amelia and her importance to the New Legionnaires. When he talks about her, he is full of pride, not even realizing that he is telling secrets that can put her life in danger. At the same time, he doesn't realize that he is making himself look weaker by the minute.

The question on the ladies' mind is, "if Iris is so great, why is she not the leader?"

Of course, they keep it to themselves. Instead, a lady asks, "Are you two close?"

"Now, we are. We didn't grow up together, but we are making up for lost time. Owen there is my other brother. He's great, too. All three of us grew up with our mothers," Russell says. Then, he puts his hand by his mouth and whispers, "We all have different mothers, but the same father. Get it?"

"Wow, your father is such a lady's man."

"He is, isn't he? I wish I could be more like him rather be so uptight. Too bad he is dead. I never got a chance to really know him as a father."

"Oh, I am so sorry to hear that. Who was he?"

Russell does not hesitate to talk about the late sovereign of Balavan and all of the sordid particulars about his corruption. While Russell happily reveals everything about himself and his family members, Nimue's ladies are busy writing them all down. Getting secrets from him is literally like taking candy from a baby. Looking over to the other two members of his team, they are also so wasted that they have no idea where they are or what they are doing.

While one of the ladies is getting intimate details about David Carson and his offspring that no one outside of the family knows, another is getting Owen to talk about his homeland. Being a former school teacher, Owen has lots of stories about Balavan and the Desiderios. While his stories are not anywhere as salacious as Russell's, the ladies are still fascinated by them. The more interested they look, the more he says. He tells the tales of el Diablo's bravery and the Warrior's tenacity on the battlefield. It's almost as if Owen is promoting the Desiderios more than his own group.

Then, one of the ladies asks the question that is on every other lady's mind, "What about the La Rivincita?"

"What about them?"

"Them? I thought that is what you call your new group."

"Oh, yes, yes. *We* are still new. There really isn't much to tell. We have a long way to go if we are going to win any battles, if you know what I mean," Owen says he hiccups a little.

The ladies cannot believe that he just admitted that his group is completely defenseless. For a moment, they think he is just kidding.

"Oh, come on, I am sure you are selling yourselves short," one of them says teasingly.

"Nope, not at all. As you already know, Russell over there is our fearless leader. That's it. There is nothing more to tell."

While Owen is telling embarrassing tales of his own organization, Cameron is dishing out information about Fouke to a third group are ladies.

"So, I hear that this Major Fouke is a dangerous man," another lady proclaims.

"Yes, he is actually a mean guy," Cameron admits while sipping more of the bubbling champagne.

"So, why are you here to rescue him if he is such a bad man?"

"It depends on who you ask!" Cameron says as he laughs raucously.

"How many versions are there?"

"Well, there's the Legionnaires version, the Desiderio's version, and our version," Cameron says as he counts with his fingers.

Then, Cameron goes into details about how he manipulates everyone to the point where even the former members of the Legionnaires despise him. The version for the Desiderios is even more dismal. He is painted as a coward as well as a murderer, two of the worst things that a soldier wants to be known for, all rolled up in one. Then, he spews out the third version. Considering that they are here to bring him back, the ladies are expecting a glorious version that highlights his heroism or perhaps tells the story about how he is misunderstood. To their surprise, it is more inglorious than anything else.

Basically, they have no intention of making him their leader. They only want his name. By saying that he is backing them, Russell and his team of inexperienced leaders will have a stronger foothold to recruit more men for their cause. When the ladies hear his tale, every one of them has an appalled look on their faces. It's as if with one short narrative, Cameron has single-handedly destroyed everything Fouke has built over the last few months. By the time the afternoon is over, the ladies already know everything they want to know from all three men.

*

While the three unsuspecting fools are mouthing off, it doesn't take long for Fouke to find them. As soon as he sees them through the window, Fouke is sickened, but he is not sure what makes him livider, the fact that these losers

157

are here to rescue him or to capture him. In either case, he can tell that they are too self-absorbed at the moment to care about their surroundings, let along the object of their mission. If he wanted to, he can kill them right now and get away with it, but he decides that these clowns are not worth the time. After all the trouble he has gone through to get the islanders to like him, he is not about to waste their good will on these three.

Just when he is about to leave in disgust, he is about to get even angrier than he already is when he hears his own name being mentioned. As he looks inside, he sees Cameron talking about him as if he is the worst piece of trash in the world. At least, he has verified with his own eyes and ears that there are indeed three incompetent men from Balavan who are here for him, but they are no friend of his. He has made his decision.

There is no way he is returning with them. If they are here to capture him, he is going to have to neutralize them. If they are here to rescue him, he is going to find a tactful way to turn them away and discredit them in order to rebuild his reputation, or whatever he has left once they are done disparaging him. With these clowns, he is sure he will be captured one way or another by Violet and Trip the instant they step foot on Balavan and paraded around town in disgrace.

"How revolting!" Fouke laments to himself as he shakes his head.

These idiots are exposing him simply because they have had a few drinks in them. They have no tact and cannot think on their feet. Their enemies can hear them from miles away. Anyone stupid enough to trust them will be dragged down with them. The question for Fouke now is how to avoid them until he comes up with a better plan. It's not going to be easy. Simply hiding in the woods will not work because he has already heard the villagers say that the chief wants him off of the island.

The only things he can think of is joining forces with the chief's advisers and trying to convince them to help him out. If he can show them that they are better off with him on their side, they will be willing to help him persuade the chief to keep him on the island. If all goes well, he is hoping that he can join them on the chief's council.

Who knows? In time, he may be able to get the chief to fight for him. But, that's for later. Now, he has to concentrate on the council members. He has already won the hearts of the villagers. Based on the rumors, the advisors are just as empty-headed as the rest of them. It should be easy to sway them.

Without a moment to lose, he scopes out the advisors, one at a time. They all appear to be drones – one looking exactly like the other. They are all men and dressed alike. When they parade around the streets, they act like they are the most important people on the island. The other villagers greet them politely, but it's pretty obvious that very few people actually like them.

There are only two members that may be use some use to him: Nimue and Albin. Since Nimue is the chief's daughter, it is a little risky to approach her. If something goes wrong, she will immediately go to her father and it's over. That leaves only one man. He knows that Albin has a sweet spot for the princess and will do just about anything to get her. That is exactly the kind of thing he looks for when searching for a mark, a weakness that he can exploit. Seeing him sitting alone by the beach, Fouke knows that this is his golden opportunity.

Walking right up to him, Fouke forces a smile and says, "Hello, do you mind if I sit with you?"

Looking up, Albin says, "Sure, it's a free beach."

"I know we have met before, but I don't think we have ever been properly introduced. I am Gavin Anderson. How do you do?" Fouke says as he extends his hand.

Shaking his hand, Albin says, "Albin. Nice to meet you," before turning his eyes back to the ocean.

"What seems to be troubling you, Albin?"

"What else?"

"The princess?"

"See! Everyone on this island knows that I love her, even an outsider like you, but she won't give me the time of the day. What gives? Do I have a giant mole on my face that I don't know about? Do I smell? Do I give the vibe of an axe murderer? What is it about me that's just so objectionable for her to reject me every single time?"

Knowing that this is the chance to make a good impression, Fouke replies, "There is absolutely nothing wrong with you. You are tall, intelligent, handsome, and strong. What woman does not want you?"

Even though he knows that it's a blatant attempt at buttering him up, Albin can care less at the moment. He's too depressed.

"The perfect one, that's what."

"I can help you win her heart, if you will let me."

Intrigued, Albin asks, "What would you do that for me?"

"I heard that you are the one who gave me the benefit of the doubt when everyone else wants to kick me off of the island or imprison me. I just want to do this as a thank you for speaking out on my behalf," Fouke says with as sincere of a tone as he can muster.

Nodding his head, Albin replies, "That is true. I am the only one who spoke for you." Then, looking determined, he says, "What do you have in mind, Fouke?"

Inside, Fouke is laughing because he knows he has this little lovesick advisor in the palm of his hand. Outside, he has to pretend to be embarrassed for having been caught in a lie.

"I apologize for using my alias rather than my birth name. I am sure you understand, considering the position I am in. Anonymity is important for someone like me."

"Yes, yes, I understand. Well?"

"Ah, back to the beautiful princess. The way I see it, you are trying too hard."

There are those infamous words, again – *trying too hard.* Those are the same words that Nimue used. At least, it sounds like Fouke knows what he is talking about.

"And, of course, any young woman would know if you are playing hard to get, too. After all, most of them are experts at that game."

"True."

"What you need to do find out what is the most important thing to her in the world and give it to her."

Rolling his eyes, Albin says, "Well, that's not very useful information at all. I know that already, but what would that be?"

Smiling, Fouke replies, "You may be too close to see it, but the most important thing in her life is her father."

Confused, Albin says, "OK, how is that supposed to help me win her over? She already has her father by her side at all times."

Fouke cannot believe how dense this young man is. No wonder he cannot win her heart. He doesn't see what is in front of him.

"No, no, you are not going to try to *give* her own father to her. What you need to do is impress her father rather than her. From what I have seen and heard, he is already quite fond of you."

"You think so?"

"Oh, yes. You are the only advisor whom he listens to. Cannot you tell that he is frustrated with everyone else? They are all nothing but dead weights and yes men. You, on the other hand, actually tell him what you think is best for the island," Fouke says as he lays on it thick with his praise.

Smiling, Albin is glad that someone sees his contributions. With the princess always going against him in these meetings, he has wondered if he is simply wasting his breath or not. After all, a royal's words usually trumps over the commoner's, even if this commoner is the son of a valued adviser.

Reading his face, Fouke is also glad, but for a completely different reason. He is now one step closer to his goal.

Keeping the momentum going, he continues, "Now, you need to show the chief that you are even more brilliant than he has given you credit for while leaving the princess alone. That way, she can see that you have the best interest of the island in your heart, which will win your way into hers."

"What do you have in mind?" Albin asks anxiously.

"First, you need to whip the rest of the advisors into shape. Your father does not need such useless people on his council. If they refuse to change, you need to replace them."

"What are you saying? You want me to make enemies with the council members?"

"You won't be making any enemies if you do it right."

"How am I supposed to do that? Most of them have been sitting on the council before I was born. As far as they are concerned, I am just some kid who got here because of my daddy."

"You will need to approach the chief. By having his consent and royal decree, they cannot turn you away."

Hesitating a little, Albin says, "So what you are saying is that by alienating myself from everyone else on the council, I will win the chief's heart, which will ultimately get me the princess."

"Exactly."

Albin is not sure if he likes this plan. He does not like to rock the boat. That is why he is always giving people the benefit of the doubt. He is supposed to be the nice guy here. He shouldn't be one who makes any kind of demands, especially not to people who have seniority over him.

Sensing the reluctance, Fouke says, "Of course, you won't be doing it alone. I will be there to help you."

"How? You are not from here. The advisers will never listen to an outsider."

"Oh, I can be very persuasive when I need to be."

"Hmm… OK, you have convinced me," Albin says as he offers his hand to his new partner in crime.

"See, what did I tell you?" Fouke laughs as Albin joins him.

The young adviser is both excited and anxious about this latest approach to winning the love of his life.

Chapter 13: Drunken Stupor

With Russell and his men sleeping off their heavenly afternoon, the ladies relay what they have learned from the three unsuspecting men to their mistress. As she listens, Nimue cannot help but laugh at what she is hearing. Everything has worked out even better than she has imagined. While she has had faith in her ladies' ability to coerce these men to talk to them, she has never imagined that it would be that easy to find out so much details about the most intimate details of their operation, their enemies, and even their personal lives. These men must be very lonely or desperate for a beautiful woman's attention. They certainly cannot hold their liquor. That's for sure.

"Amateurs," the princess says with a huff.

With her ladies and their notes in tow, she rushes to tell her father the latest news.

"I have always known that you have the best interest of the island in your heart," the chief says as he beams with pride.

"I knew that Gavin fellow cannot be trusted."

"You mean Fouke."

"Hmph, we should just call him Scum. That name should fit him perfectly," Nimue says as she fumes.

"Now, now, it's not all that bad," the chief says trying to calm her down. Turning towards her ladies, he says, "I want to commend all of you for your excellent work!"

"Thank you, your majesty!" all three ladies say at once as they all curtsy in front of him like triplets.

"Now, if you ladies will excuse us, we have work to do."

As soon as they are alone, the chief continues, "What are you thinking right now?"

"Isn't it obvious? We should kill him."

Laughing, the chief says, "Ah, you are still young. You cannot just kill someone out of anger, my dear. Or, you will quickly find yourself feared and possibly dead."

Embarrassed, the princess says, "I am sorry, Poppy."

"That's my girl. Someday, you will rule this entire kingdom and I know you will be the best ruler this world has ever seen. Now, if you were the ruler, how would you tackle this little problem of ours – diplomatically, mind you?" the chief says with a smile.

"We should cease him and put him on trial."

"Good, good. What else? What about the three men who spilled all of their secrets?"

"They will be witnesses to his crime, of course."

"And what makes you think they will repeat everything they have said during their drunken stupor? For all we know, they won't even remember that they said all of that. We do have one of the most potent wines anywhere in the world." After a short pause, the chief continues, "You see, when you trick people into doing things the first time, they will not be so willing to fall for it again."

"What do you think we should do?"

"I think we should find out which one of the ladies these three men like. If the ladies agree to it, they should lure them to our side."

"What makes you think it will work?"

"Oh, we men are simple creatures, aren't we?" the chief says as he laughs.

Unbeknownst to the chief and the princess, Albin is right outside of the hut the entire time, listening to their conversation. He cannot believe his ears. Just minutes ago, he has agreed to be Fouke's ally in shaking up the advisers and impressing the chief. Now, he doesn't know what to do. Is Fouke really that bad of a man? He is completely conflicted. He has hoped that this is the chance that he has been waiting for to win his love's heart, but he cannot do it alone.

After what he has heard, he can no longer work with Fouke. Once she finds out that he has anything to do with him, she is going to be furious. He must cut his ties with the outsider. Even though he knows that Fouke will not be happy about it, he really has no other choice.

Right now, he has a more pressing problem. Pacing back and forth in front of the hut, Albin is not sure if he should go into the hut and act like nothing has happened or if he should confess that he has heard everything. If he chooses the former, he knows he is going down a dangerous path of lies and deceit. Since he has always prided himself in being honest, he really does not want to use that approach. Yet, can he admit that he has just eavesdropped on the chief and the princess?

It's an extremely impolite thing to do. He has not planned on doing it, but just hearing the name Fouke in their conversation piqued his interest. He has inadvertently become a snoop on his casual walk from the beach back to his hut. What makes it worse is that he is listening in on the back of the hut, instead of the front where the guards are, which makes his unintentional act of overhearing the royal's conversation sound even more shameful. By the time he realizes what he is doing, he has already heard too much and can no longer back away. Choosing to take the side of dignity, he walks to the front of the hut and knocks on the door.

"Who is it?" Nimue asks.

"It is I, Albin."

"What is he doing here?" the princess mumbles.

"Come in," the chief says.

"I was just walking by and wanted to see if you need anything," Albin asks politely.

"No, we don't," Nimue says instinctively.

"Well, we can always use hear your opinion about something," the chief says.

Nimue hates it when her father overrides her. Even though he has every right to do so both as a parent and as a chief, it still bugs her a great deal. Meanwhile, Albin is glad that he doesn't have to make his confession, quite just yet. If he gives a good answer, perhaps the chief and the princess may not take his snooping offense quite as badly.

"What do you think is the best way for a woman to get a man's heart?" the chief asks.

Upon hearing the chief, both Nimue and Albin are completely shocked. It has nothing to do with any of the intruders. Where is this question coming from? Both of them are wonder if he is insinuating that the princess may have feeling for the young adviser. At that thought Nimue is furious while Albin is completely embarrassed.

Laughing, the chief says, "I thought so."

Instantly, both youngsters realize that the chief is merely testing them. Albin takes a sigh of relief before letting out a nervous laughter.

"What are really doing here?" Nimue says angrily towards Albin.

As his heart pounds harder, he swallows hard and admits that he accidentally heard everything from outside of the hut and would like to know if there is anything he can do to help. While Nimue tries her best to hold her tongue, her anger easily shows on her face. The chief, however, is not incensed in the least bit.

"Thank you for telling us. Now, I would like for you to join our little dinner party later with the ladies."

"Of course, your majesty. Anything else?"

"Yes, next time you come around, it wouldn't hurt if you brought a gift. Isn't customary to bring something when you visit someone's house? I don't know – say, flowers or wine," the chief teases again.

"I apologies, your majesty. I will remember that next time," Albin says as he blushes, knowing full well that the chief is trying to help him out with the princess.

*

As he finally makes his way back to his hut, Albin finds that he is not alone. The door is open even though he always makes sure that it's closed. This has never happened before. Everyone on this island knows that this is his home and no one ever dares to go in it uninvited.

Taking out his dagger, he opens the door wider and says, "Who's there?"

Not hearing anything, he walks inside the door. Then, sniff, sniff. He smells something good coming from the kitchen.

"What in the world?" Albin asks himself.

As he keeps his dagger drawn, he slowly walks towards the source of the aroma.

"Hey, there, friend!" Fouke says as he turns around and smiles at him.

"What are you doing in my house?" Albin asks as he puts his dagger back in.

"I wanted to help you make some of my best dishes so you can impress the princess."

"What is it?"

"It's a special dish from Balavan that is often served on special occasions, like weddings and birthdays."

"The princess and I already have plans."

"Really?!? Congratulations!" Fouke exclaims.

Realizing that the words didn't come out quite right, Albin tries to correct himself.

"No, no, that's not what I meant! I meant we have official business to attend to tonight with many others. It's not a date!"

"Oh, but, you can make it into one, if you know what you are doing!"

Albin cannot believe that this is the same man that Nimue's ladies were talking about. How can he be evil? He has helped so many villagers since he has been here. Now, he seems genuinely trying to help him win the princess's heart. How can anyone be such a good actor if he is such a wicked man?

Ignoring his own instinct for the moment, Albin leans over the stove and takes a big whiff.

"It smells delicious. What is it?"

"It's a combination of all of the finest ingredients in the area. It has octopus, squid, trout, clams, oysters, and lobsters, as well as coconuts, banana leaves, and orange peels, but the star of the show is a secret ingredient that I brought with me."

Reaching into his pocket, Fouke takes out a vile of orange liquid and says, "Just a small dash will do."

As he throws it in, Albin can instantly smell the heavenly scent coming from the pot. It is absolutely delicious as he starts to salivate unintentionally.

"Isn't it absolutely delectable?" Fouke asks.

Even though his mouth wants to taste it, his brain tells him not to. After all, a part of him cannot help but wonder if Fouke is trying to poison him. If he is such a criminal, he has to have something hidden up his sleeves. After all, he did enter his house uninvited. Even though it's not locked, he shouldn't have just helped himself to another man's home like that. Knowing what he is thinking, Fouke takes a ladle and sips the soup to show his skeptical host that there is nothing to fear.

"Ah, perfect!" he says as he pats himself in the back.

Then, Albin's stomach lets out a big growl.

Laughing, Fouke says, "Come one, don't torture yourself."

Taking out two bowls, he gives them both big heaping helpings of the freshly made stew. He also takes out two wine glasses and fills it up with wine.

"Where did you get the ingredients for all this? I don't remember having them," Albin mumbles with his mouth full.

"Oh, I caught them fresh this morning at the beach. Why do you think I was there?" Fouke asks.

It's a good excuse, which is perfect for covering up his true intentions. Without it, his *chance* meeting at the beach may seem a little creepy to some. Albin seems to have bought it as he nods.

After he is done savoring every morsel, Albin says, "Thank you, it is absolutely delightful."

Reaching into his pocket and retrieving the vial, Fouke says, "Here, take it. You can make one for yourself anytime."

"Oh, I couldn't possibly."

"No, it's OK. I know where to find them back in Balavan."

Not to seem ungrateful, Albin accepts.

"Well, I got to go. In the meantime, you should try to make the dish yourself. If you like it as much as I think you do, I am sure your princess will, too," Fouke says with a smile.

"OK, thanks."

With that, Fouke smiles and takes his leave. He is glad that he still has Albin in his back pocket, but that is not the only reason. Unbeknownst to Albin, he actually gave him a different vile than the one he cooked with.

While this one looks and even smells exactly the same, it is as Albin had feared before – it is laced with poison. Looking at the vile, he wonders what ingredient is in it that makes it so appetizing. He has to find out so he can reproduce it later. After all, it's not a very big vile. If he is to throw a feast to impress the princess and the chief, he will need a lot more of it than what he has. Opening a cabinet in his kitchen, he puts it in the front and decides to find out another day.

*

Fouke is now on full offensive. He knows that Albin will use that vial someday. If it's not now, it will happen soon. He knows an infatuated puppy like him cannot resist offering a home cooked meal to a loved one. And, when he does, he is hoping that he will kill the chief and the princess

171

all in one fell swoop. Then, he can take over the island as its new leader with Albin taking the blame for the murders. After all, the other advisors on the council are all too weak to resist.

Then, he moves to Russell and his men. Still sleeping, the men are alone as all of the ladies have left, taking their gadgets and tools with them. Unguarded, Fouke walks in. Cameron is snoring on the floor while Russell is lying on the bed hugging a pillow like a child. On the sofa is Owen who is in deep sleep as he takes long breathes that are easily audible. All three men are barely dressed with nothing but a pair of trousers on. It is clear to see that none of them has any weapons on them.

"This is just too easy," Fouke says as he shakes his head.

Putting on a pair of gloves, he takes out a dagger from his belt, wipes it clean with his jacket and plunges it into Owen's heart, killing him before the poor man has a chance to utter a sound.

Then, he puts the dagger in Cameron's right hand before returning to Nonni and Grami's hut.

"Where have you been, Gavin?" Nonni asks when she sees him coming.

"Oh, I have been helping some of the ladies across the street," Fouke says. Knowing that the generic answer is not going to appease her, he reaches into his bag and says, "I also went fishing."

Taking out the variety of catches ranging from the more common fish like trout and tuna to the more exotic creatures like octopus, squid, and sea urchin, Fouke says, "I thought you ladies might want to try some of this nice fresh seafood tonight."

Smiling, Nonni is delighted with his offerings. They all look very fresh and large. It's as if they are all in season. The timing is perfect. Nonni just ran out of fresh seafood and she was about to go to the market to get some more. Fouke is glad that he has also diffused her. She looks too preoccupied with the fish to suspect that he has been involved in any form of foul play. Then, he offers to help in the kitchen, which Nonni happily accepted.

Meanwhile, Nimue is sending three of her ladies to fetch their honored guests, one for each man. During the private dinner party, she intends on getting Russell and his men to admit that Fouke is a fraud, whereby giving them the authority to imprison him before he causes any real damage, not realizing that trouble has already begun. As soon as they enter the room, they scream as they see the grizzly sight.

"What? What happened?" Cameron says as he is jerked awake by the sound of shrieking.

As he blinks and struggles to see what is going on through his throbbing head, he realizes that he is holding on to something. Looking to his right hand, he realizes that there is a bloody dagger in his hand.

"What in the world?" Cameron says as he drops the weapon.

As the sound of the clank when the dagger hits the ground, the ladies all look at him in shock. Then, they run back towards the chief's hut as quickly as they can.

"Wait! Wait! This is not what it looks like!" Cameron shouts.

With all of the commotion, Russell is also waking up.

"What is going on? Why is everyone shouting? What time is it?" Russell says as he sits up on the bed.

As he focuses on the floor, he cannot believe his eyes. He robs them again just to be sure that he is actually seeing what he is seeing.

"Is, is that blood?" Russell shouts.

"What? Where?" Cameron asks as he is still quite groggy from the effects of the alcohol.

Jumping up from the bed, Russell shouts, "There! That!"

Then, hopping off of the bed, he runs towards his brother who is lying in a pool of his own blood with his eyes still firmly closed.

"Who did this?! Who killed my brother?!?" Russell shouts as he rocks him in his arms. "Did you see anyone? What happened?" Russell continues to shout.

Terrified, Cameron doesn't know what to think. Despite his imposingly large size, he has never hurt anyone before, let alone killing anyone or anything for that matter. If he can help it, he prefers to throw them outside than to kill even pests like mosquitos and spiders. Now that he is looking at the blood on his hand left by the dagger, he starts to go into shock.

Going into fetal position, he starts to rock himself. Then, he looks at his legs. He has inadvertently wiped the blood from his hand to his knees when he hugged them.

Jumping up, he goes straight to the lavatory to wash everything off, but even after a dozen washes, it doesn't seem to come off. The stench of the blood still seems to fill the air. The red stain seems to stay no matter how hard he scrubs it. Before he knows it, he has scratched his hands and knees raw to the point that it starts to bleed. The sight of more blood only prompts him to scrub even harder.

As if things cannot get any worse for the poor giant, Nimue's ladies have brought a dozen armed guards with her. Within minutes, they storm the lavatory and capture him.

Puzzled, Russell shouts, "Wait, why are you taking him away? Wait! Stop!"

As the guards completely ignore his plea as they push him aside, Russell doesn't know what to think. What is going on? Who are these people? Why are these men armed? Why won't they listen to me? Why are they … Then, he looks at the blood that is still on Cameron's arms and legs and looks down at the limp lifeless body of his brother. Suddenly, he realizes what is going on.

Even though the blood is Cameron's own, Russell doesn't know that. The truth of the matter is it makes no difference. As he watches the ladies recount seeing Cameron with the bloody dagger in his hand, Russell reluctantly puts two and two together. Cameron must have killed Owen. Judging from the evidence stacked against him, there seems to be good enough proof for anyone.

"You?! Why!?!" Russell screams as he rushes Cameron like an undisciplined teenage boy.

The guards immediately hold him back before he gets the chance to slug him in the face.

One of them coldly says, "You need to back away. He is now in our custody."

Dazed, Russell doesn't know what to think. He plops down on the ground next to his brother's corpse and simply stares into thin air. He cannot figure out what happened. Just an hour ago, they were all so happy, all three of them. At least, he thinks they were. Even though he remembers being elated, he has no idea what happened exactly. Everything is a little foggy as his head continues to thump.

He remembers eating and drinking a lot, but cannot remember what he ate. Was it turkey or pork? Or, was it fish? He remembers enjoying taking every bite, but cannot remember what was so good about it. Was the food sweet, salty, or spicy? He has no clue. He remembers cracking jokes, but doesn't know what he said. He remembers being surrounded by people, but cannot remember a single face. This is bad – very bad.

He has to try. Hitting the side of his head, he has to get himself to sober up, but he cannot. Nothing is coming to him. How and when did his brother die? He doesn't remember a single moment when there was a struggle. There were no signs of distress or was there? He vaguely remembers Owen laughing and saying things to the ladies, but all he remembers hearing are muffled sounds of blah, blah, blah intermingled with sounds of giggling.

What about Cameron? What was he doing? All Russell can remember is that he was doing pretty much the same thing as Owen, just in the other side of the room. He doesn't remember Cameron getting anywhere near Owen or even speaking to him from across the room. He was too into his own conversations to care about what the other two were doing, just like Russell himself. In fact, he vaguely remembers that Cameron was facing a different direction from his brother. There was no way they had a disagreement that would have caused him to kill him.

Then again, Russell doesn't remember seeing the ladies leave. He must have passed out before that happened. If so, did the ladies commit the murder and frame Cameron for the crime? It's definitely a possibility. He doesn't know them at all. Any of them can have a problem with outsiders and take the matter into their own hands.

Looking at their petrified faces, however, Russell wonders if any of them could be the culprit. They don't look like spies who are masters at acting. All three of them look genuinely scared to see the dead body.

Maybe, it's worse than that. Maybe, their mistress gave them to command to do it? Even though she seems like a lovely woman, he doesn't know her either. If he did, however, Russell knows that all three of them are doomed.

176

Why stop at one if you want to rid the island of all outsiders? Swallowing hard, Russell is getting more horrified by the second. He knows he is way over his head and things are getting out of hand fast.

Meanwhile, Cameron's face is pale and terrified. This is not what he signed up for when he agreed to be a part of Russell's team. He was going to use his skills as a translator to help them negotiate with the locals and bring back Fouke. It was supposed to be a quick and easy adventure, one that he was excited to participate in. He never had that chance to use his talents.

Instead, he is being accused of something so heinous that no one who knows him would ever believe it. Yet, there he is. He is being shackled for murdering his friend, a harmless school teacher who has never done anything evil in his life. Never once has he ever imagined that he would be in this situation. He would rather kill himself than another fellow human being.

The worst thing is he is starting to wonder if he actually did it. Since he cannot remember what happened after passing out, he wonders if somehow he did kill Owen but doesn't realize it. Does he have a dark hidden side that he does not know? He prays that he doesn't.

Nevertheless, no matter how ridiculous it sounds, but he cannot help feel that there may be some truth to it.

Chapter 14: The Trial

All along the island, word is spreading quickly. Rumor has it that there is a murder on the island, the first one in thirty years. Everyone is whispering in shock as they shake their heads in disbelief. Meanwhile, Fouke is inside Nonni and Grami's hut, acting as if nothing has happened. The only hint that he knows anything about what is going on is a very faint smile in the corner of his mouth.

With the new turn of events, everything is turned upside down on the once peaceful, albeit infamous, Trozos Island. The private dinner for the honored guests has been canceled. In its place is a murder trial, one that is so unconscionable that no one can believe it is happening. How can anyone murder a friend in cold blood? It is certainly not something that any of the locals has ever seen before. The last murder on the island occurred out of passion. A man caught his wife with another man and snapped. It was a huge debacle at the time, but it was nothing compared to this one.

Unlike that murder, there does not seem to be a motive for Cameron to kill Owen. They seemed to have been close friends and comrades. No one saw any inkling of violent in the murderer before or after his arrest. Even now, he seems to be in mourning than anything else. In fact, there seems to be tears in his eyes, but it's so faint that it's hard to tell. It just looks like his eyes are glistening in the sun. For those who can see inside those eyes, however, they can see a man deeply distressed, not because of the predicament that he is in, but for the poor man who has lost his life.

Nevertheless, that doesn't stop the onlookers from thinking of the worst. Before this tragedy, people generally left their doors open and let their children play on the streets. In fact, some of the residents don't even have windows. On the island, the temperature is always mild enough to not need them, allowing them to enjoy the fresh air and the sound of nature to immerse their homes at all time. Now, many of the islanders are starting to feel unsafe for the first time in their lives. They are pulling their children closer to them. Some are even hiding inside their huts with everything firmly shut. The atmosphere in the air has also turned foul. It seems even the native animals seem to know that something is up as they seem to stay at a distance.

Because crime is so rare on the island, there is no prison per se. The only thing they have to use for such a nefarious occasion is a small storage hut that they have emptied out just an hour earlier when the ladies frantically reported the murder. As Cameron is being led to the makeshift prison, he hangs his head low, too ashamed to look at the people who are staring at him in disgust, judging him before he gets a chance to defend himself from the unthinkable crime. Everyone from young toddlers to the elderly women are pointing their fingers at him and whispering.

"Have you heard what happened?" Nonni says to Fouke as the guards pass by her hut.

"I heard something about a murder. Is that right?" Fouke replies with a curious look on his face.

"Yes. Apparently, one of the fellows who just came ashore killed one of the other fellows who came with him. Isn't that the most bizarre thing you have ever heard?"

"Wow, that's so sad! Wonder what happened?" Fouke feigns concern.

"Don't know. Whatever it is, it sure looks pretty ugly. Are you going to go see the trial?"

"Oh, no, I cannot possibly."

"Why not?"

"I don't feel comfortable going to a murder trial. It gives me the creeps to see someone who may be a killer," Fouke says as he fakes a shudder.

Nonni looks at him with a smile and says, "I understand. I will be going if you change your mind. I am sure the entire island will turn up for the trial. I would love for you to join me."

"I hate to disappoint you, but I really don't want to be there, but I will keep that in mind."

Of course, Fouke will be at the trial, but he certainly is not about to let anyone else know that. Like any other criminal who has framed another, he wants to know every little detail of the trial so he knows that the poor scapegoat will take the full blame for it. At the same time, he plans on going in and out of the trial any time he needs to in case something goes wrong. For example, Cameron can tell the entire village about Fouke and expose him to everyone. If that's the case, he may not have a choice but to flee, but he is betting that the timid Cameron will just fold instead of trying to blame someone else.

Besides, he is still Gavin Anderson to most of the people on the island, even though he knows that the chief and his advisors know better. For whatever reason, they are keeping that to themselves right now, which suits him just fine. He needs to keep up his persona as a helpful but passive outsider who is trying to stay under the radar. On the other hand, by keeping the option of going with her open, he has an excuse if someone happens to see him there.

*

At dawn the next morning, everyone is gathered in the center of the island to watch the spectacle of the century. Locked in a wooden cage made out of palm trees, Cameron looks absolutely defeated as he stands there looking like an abandoned puppy that has been thrown in a shelter. The only difference is, unlike the puppies that search eagerly in the sea of the onlookers for someone to love him; he knows that no one is coming for him.

As the chief and the princess sit down at the throne, his guard captain stands up and loudly announces, "We are here to conduct the murder trial of Owen Brown. The accused is Cameron Temple. How do you plea?"

As usual, the princess translates afterwards.

After a short pause, Cameron says, "Not guilty" in perfect Trozian.

The crowd is amazed and shocked at the same time. Beside Fouke, no one has ever heard an outsider speak their language before. Until today, none of them even thought that any outsider even knows what their language sounds like without setting foot on the island first. Being isolated from everyone else, the language is quite unique and difficult to learn. After living with them for months and interacting with them on a daily basis, Fouke knew the basics and could understand them, but he constantly mispronounced many words due to his accent. He did understand everything else they were saying, though.

After realizing that he speaks their native tongue fluently, some of the islanders are a little embarrassed. If they had known that he understands what they are saying, they would not have been so brutal and vocal in their criticism of him when he was paraded through the island the previous day. After all, these are supposed to be nice and polite people. Even though they do it all the time, they know very well that talking behind people's back is definitely rude. But, what's done is done.

181

Like everyone else, the chief is surprised.

"How did you learn our language?" he asks curiously

"I am a student of cultures and linguistics. I have always been intrigued by anyone from a different land and have made a point of studying from them ever since I was a child."

"Who exactly did you learn Trozian from?" the chief asks as the entire crowd hushes in anticipation of his answer.

"I don't recall. I traveled to many different lands when I was young."

While the chief wants to believe him, it's kind of difficult to do so. Considering how fluent he is, there is no way it is simply a language that he happens to have picked up along the way during one of his many travels as a child. No one can be *that* good at a language without being able to practice it with someone else on a regular basis. Like everything else in life, being able to speak a language is a skill that gets rusty with time if unused.

"Who do you speak the language with back home?"

"No one."

"Then, how do you keep up with it?"

Looking a little embarrassed, he looks down and whispers, "I practice in front of a mirror."

"What?"

Clearing his throat, he repeats a little louder, "I... I practice in front of a mirror."

Upon hearing those words, the crowd cannot help but laugh.

Hushing everyone, the chief says, "Do you do that with every language you know?"

"Yes."

"How many languages do you know?"

Using his fingers to count as he thinks for a minute, he says, "Twelve."

There is an instant sound of gasping in the crowd. Everyone is instantly awestruck by this man. No one can believe that a big brutish man like this is such a refined linguist.

The chief then says, "Well, even though I am very impressed with your skills, you still stand accused of murder. Let's not waste any more time. I want to hear from your own words, what were you doing when the victim was killed?"

"I was asleep along with the deceased and my friend Russell."

Not knowing what to do or think, Russell is standing by a nearly hut, trying to stay away from it all, but cannot get himself to. Even though he does not understand a word, he definitely recognizes his own name being uttered by his friend as everyone stares at him.

"How do you explain the bloody knife in your hand if you were asleep?" the chief asks as the guard shows the knife to the crowd – still with Owen's blood on it.

The crowd look disgusted at the murder weapon while some of them cover their eyes to try to avoid the sight of blood. It's one thing to see blood when preparing a chicken for dinner. It's totally another to see blood from a human being.

"I cannot. I don't know where the knife came from."

"So, you deny that it's yours."

"Yes."

"So, enlighten me. Who do you think may have put the knife in your hand while you were sleep?"

"I don't know."

"Do you have any idea who this knife may belong to?"

"No. I have never seen it before in my life. I didn't bring one with me either."

As the guard brings the knife closer, the chief says, "Look closely."

At first, Cameron hesitates to look, because he too, does not like the sight of blood. But, as the guard pushes it closer to his face, he has no choice but to look at it. If he doesn't, he is afraid that the guard will push it so close that it will actually touch his face. Just the thought of having Owen's blood on his face makes him retch just a little bit.

Upon studying the dagger, it looks quite exquisite. Despite the blood stains, it's plain to see that it has an extremely sharp blade with a perfectly smooth edge. The grip is wrapped tightly with simple brown rawhide. He can still smell the fresh scent of new leather on it. It looks and smells almost brand new; as if this is the only time it has been used. The pommel is perfectly round with a small ruby embedded in it on one side and a small sapphire on the other. It doesn't look like an ordinary dagger. It certainly doesn't look like a common islander can afford something like this. He himself cannot afford a dagger like this.

Shaking his head, he says, "No, I don't know whose knife it is."

"This is not looking good for you. You are not helping yourself with these answers. I suggest you give me something I can work with or you are out of luck."

"I am sorry, your majesty. I really don't know. The only people I know on this island are Russell and…" Cameron's voice cracks a little before as he finally utters, "Owen."

184

Taking a deep breath, Cameron continues, "I have never seen either one of them with that dagger. I don't know anyone else on this island well enough to know what kind of dagger they have. The only people I spent time with are the ladies that the princess sent to our hut this afternoon, but I don't think any of them carried any type of weapons with them. The only thing that even resembles a dagger is a small file that they used to clean our nails. Besides, I cannot imagine any of them want to do me or my friends any harm. I didn't see anyone else in the hut before I fell asleep."

The crowd gasp again as they whisper to one another. This is definitely gossip worthy. Despite having heard the rumors, the islanders cannot believe that he has confirmed that the princess has sent them her ladies for an afternoon of pampering. This is a treatment that is reserved for the highest of dignitary and is rarely talked about. It is definitely a rare luxury.

At the same time, Nimue heard something else. Even though it is not his intention, Cameron has pointed his fingers at her ladies when he placed them at the murder scene. The young princess is visibly upset next to the chief. She knows exactly what he is implying and what the crowd is thinking.

"This is preposterous!" the princess stands up and says. "Is he accusing my ladies of something? If he is, why doesn't he come out and say it?"

The chief puts his hand down and says, "Please."

Nimue grudgingly sits back down as the chief says, "Well? Answer the princess. Are you making an accusation?"

Waving his hand, Cameron says, "Oh, no, your majesty! I wouldn't possibly accuse the lovely ladies of any wrongdoing! That is not what I was saying at all."

"But you are saying that they are the last ones to see the victim alive since you and your friends fell asleep before they left."

Even though he knows the answer is yes, he doesn't want to say it. As much as he doesn't want to be falsely accused, he has no intention of placing the blame on them either.

"Well?" the chief asks impatiently.

Nodding his head, Cameron keeps his eyes on the ground.

Nodding at the guards, they immediately go towards the ladies to detain them.

"Oh, no, you wouldn't dare!" Nimue says as she stands between the guards and her ladies, some of whom are shivering in fear and crying.

The chief says, "You need to move, princess. They are not under arrest. I just want to hear their side of the story."

As the guards put them in front of the chief, the ladies are beyond terrified as they huddle together.

Pointing at the only girl who is still composed, the chief says, "OK, tell me your story?"

The lady says, "After we treat the gentlemen to an afternoon of pampering, all three of them fell asleep. That is when we all left."

"Did you see anyone enter the room when you left?"

"No, your majesty."

"Did you see anyone suspicious around the hut?"

"No, your majesty."

"How did you leave the men when you left?"

"Just as they lie. One of the men was on the bed. Another was on the sofa. And, the third one was on the floor."

"Did you see this knife the entire time you were in the room?"

Taking a deep breath, the lady studies the dagger before saying, "No, your majesty."

Even though she says no, there is a twinkle in her eye that caught the chief's attention.

"But, you recognize this dagger, don't you?" the chief asks.

Nodding, the lady admits it.

The crowd gasps again. They have not been this entertained in a very long time.

"Where?" the chief continues.

"I believe this dagger belongs to Albin."

There is a complete silence in the crowd. Before, they are amused. Now, they are concerned. They all know what she is saying. She is now accusing Albin, the chief's advisor and the princess's love interest, of this murder. Of course, no one is as surprised as Albin when he heard his name being uttered during the trial. From where he is standing, he cannot get a good look at the murder weapon. Despite being there since the beginning of the trial, he had no idea that it belonged to him.

Hiding in a tall tree, Fouke is watching the entire trial from a bird's eye view and totally enjoying every moment of it.

He is having so much fun that tears are coming down as he tries to quiet his laughter.

"Ah, they make it *so* easy!" Fouke says to himself.

When he went into Albin's house earlier, he stole one of his many daggers for this occasion. He wanted to take one that is plain enough to be innocuous but with just a hint of elegance so someone will recognize it. This trial has proven him right.

The chief nods towards a guard who goes and apprehends Albin just like he did with the ladies.

"Is this your knife?" the chief asks as the guard displays it in front of him.

Looking at the dagger closely, he knows it is. He had it made especially for Princess Nimue, but didn't have the nerve to give it to her. From a distance, the dagger is designed to appear to be ordinary but flawless, because he wants to show her that, to the outside world, he wants a perfect relationship like any other couple in love. Upon closer inspection, however, the dagger is anything but bland because he wants to tell her that their relationship is much deeper than it appears. The red ruby is supposed to symbolize his love for her and the blue sapphire represents his undying friendship and loyalty. The tight binding of the leather signifies the tight kinship he feels when he is with her.

Since he has invited Nimue and her ladies to his hut before, he is not surprised that one of them recognizes it. Being a naturally suspicious person, he is sure that she had the ladies check out his hut to make sure that everything is safe. Besides that, very few people have ever laid eyes on it before. Albin wonders how his precious dagger ended up in the hands of a murder suspect. He has never taken it out of his hut before, but at the same time, he has never bothered to hide it. It simply sits on his night stand by his bed so he can look at it every day and keep it close to him when he sleeps. He remembers seeing it this morning when he woke up at dawn, but hasn't seen it since. Someone must have stolen it that day after he left.

"Who could have done such a thing?" Albin asks himself as he digs to the back of his head and replay the events of the day.

It doesn't take him long to think of the answer – Fouke. He was in his hut that afternoon to make him his famous Balavian dish. Yet, the kind side of him tells him that there is a good six hours between the time he saw it last and when Fouke was in his hut. Anyone could have walked in during that time.

"Did he take it? Why would he? I thought he wants to help me win the princess's heart? Or, is it all a trick to frame me?" Albin laments.

"Answer the question," the chief demands, interrupting his thought.

Nodding, Albin admits, "Yes, Sire, it is."

"Do you have anything to do with the murder?"

"No, of course not, Sire!" Albin says fervently.

"Where were you this afternoon?"

"I was at the beach in the first part of the afternoon. Then, I was at your hut, you majesty, before going back home."

Nodding, the chief remembers that the eavesdropping incident outside of his hut around the time of the murder. What better alibi can he have than to be with the chief himself? Nevertheless, he wants to be thorough so no one can accuse him of being biased. After all, many people are pretty sure that Albin will be his son-in-law one day. It may not be soon, but it will most certainly happen.

"Did anyone see you at the beach?" the chief asks.

Hesitating, Albin does not want to tell him that he was there with Fouke because he doesn't want anyone to know about their conversation. At the same time, he doesn't want to lie to the chief, in front of the princess, no less.

"Yes, I was there with Gavin Anderson."

Then, the chief asks the question that he dreads the most. "What were you talking about?"

Fidgeting, he mumbles, "I would rather not say."

"This is a murder trial. You will answer the question."

"I am sorry, your majesty, but it's personal. I assure you that it has nothing to do with the defendant or the deceased as I did not know them."

Hearing those words, Nimue knows instantly that he was talking about her. While she is curious as to what he said, she certainly does not want anyone else to know.

"Your majesty, I think his answer is satisfactory."

Nodding, the chief understands what she means. He does not want to embarrass her any more than she does.

Taking a sigh of relief, Albin says, "Thank you, your majesty."

"Don't thank me yet. I am not done with you," the chief snaps.

If Albin doesn't look like he has just gotten away with anything, the chief would not let him go then and there, but not anymore. Chief Cai hates it when people assume that he is easing up on them or giving up on anything. It doesn't matter what the situation is or how trial it may seem to anyone else. It's like his pet peeve. He thinks it makes him look weak in front of everyone else.

"While I agree with the princess that you do not need to divulge the details of your conversation if it is so personal, I still want to know why you were having a conversation at the beach alone with an outsider. Are you teaming up with him to plot against the island?"

Waving his hand frantically, Albin vehemently denies it.

"No, Sire, I couldn't possibly. I love Trozos with all my heart and the people living on it! I assure you it was not a planned meeting, sire. I was merely taking a break by coming to the beach to clear my head. I believe Gavin was there to catch some fish for dinner."

Seeing that Albin is once again terrified, the chief is now satisfied.

Returning to the subject of the murder weapon, the chief says, "If you are confirming that this knife is yours, how do you explain how it ended up at the scene of the crime?"

"I cannot. The only thing I can think of is that someone stole it."

Once again, the crowd gasps. Even though it is the most logical explanation, none of the islanders want to admit that someone can actually steal something from one of their own. It's such an unconscionable thing to do. Although it is nothing compared to a murder, a crime is still a crime on the island. In the eyes of the locals, taking something without permission is almost as bad as taking someone's life or child. It seems the entire island is falling apart. If the air is not already thick enough, it has just gotten thicker.

"Do you have anyone in mind?"

While a part of him desperately wants to point his finger at Fouke, a larger part of him tells him to hold his tongue at all cost. Without proof, he simply cannot place the blame on another human being no matter how much his guts tells him to, especially in public and in front of the entire village. He certainly doesn't want to be blamed for something he hasn't done. Ironically, there he is, being interrogated for something he *hasn't* done.

Sadly, Fouke knows that. That is one of the many reasons that he targeted Albin in the first place. He is too kind hearted and too optimistic to rat him or anyone else out without irrefutable proof of guilt.

Shaking his head, Albin finally answers the question.

"OK, you may go now," the chief says.

Turning his attention back to Cameron, the chief focuses his attention to the primary suspect. Going over the same questions repeatedly, he continues to interrogate the poor man who had nothing but water to drink for the last five hours.

Where were you when Owen was killed? How did the blood get on your hands? Did you see anyone in the room? Who were the last people to see Owen alive? Do you sleepwalk? What time was it when you fell asleep? Did you fall sleep before or after the victim? What about your other friend Russell? What do you remember him doing at the time of the murder? Do you hold any grudge against the victim? How well do you know Owen? What about Russell?

With each question, Cameron looks more and more distraught. So much so that he does not even realize that he is starving. Even though he has not had anything to eat since the little feast that Nimue's ladies have thrown them on the prior day, food is the last thing on his mind right now. What is bothering him most is his self-doubt. As expected, he is also getting less sure of his answers. In fact, this line of questioning is getting him to doubt himself again. Since he has always lived alone, he has no idea whether or not he sleepwalks? Is it possible for him to sleep *kill*? He doesn't think so. He doesn't know of anyone in his family who sleepwalks and has never been told that he does, but that doesn't mean that he doesn't.

Despite being winded after hours of interrogation, the trial continues. As the chief takes a breather, the captain of the guards has taken over the responsibility of asking, or rather reiterating the questions in different ways. By now, it has gotten so redundant that the spectators have started to leave. Before long, there are only a handful of people left, one of which is Russell. After watching the entire trial from a distance, he is more convinced than ever that Cameron has been framed.

Without knowing the chief or the people, however, anyone can be a suspect. Russell is starting to wonder if Torgny had sent him there intentionally, expecting this murder to take place. Did the nice elderly spy who appeared to want to help him capture Fouke set him up? Did the chief put him up to it? Is there an underground element here at work? Russell doesn't have an answer, but he is certainly not about to let his poor friend take the fall if this was all an elaborate scheme to destroy them.

Chapter 15: Searching for Clues

As he walks away from the center of attention, however, Nimue knows that Albin does have a suspect in mind. Even though she does not admit it, she knows him better than anyone else. She can tell from his expression that he is conflicted because he does not want to hurt someone else.

"Hey, hold up!" Nimue says as she gets up to meet him.

"Hello, princess. It's wonderful to see you," Albin says with a smile.

No matter the situation, he is always glad to see her. Even if she is yelling from the top of her lungs, he still finds her absolutely adorable.

"Are you ok?" the princess asks.

Smiling, Albin says, "Of course, why wouldn't I be?"

He knows very well that this is not a social call, but he doesn't care. It doesn't faze him one bit to know that she intends on asking him more about his knife and his whereabouts.

Without wasting another word, she comes out and asks, "So, what did you and Gavin talk about?"

Smiling, he says, "You."

"What about me?"

"Just how obvious it is that I am in love with you."

Irritated, Nimue says, "What else?"

Not wanting to get into too much detail without lying, he says, "Nothing much. He was just offering his assistance."

Intrigued, she asks, "Assistance for what?"

"For getting your attention," Albin answers as he blushes a little.

"Why is he offering you this assistance?" she asks with skepticism as she ignores the fact that his face is turning in the shade of a tomato.

"I think it's because I spoke on his behalf when he first arrived," Albin responds truthfully.

A part of him is wondering why she is so comfortable asking the question. He was sure that she would be a little bit embarrassed to know that they were talking about how best to win her over. What he doesn't realize is that while most women may think his conversation with Gavin is nothing more than a romantic gesture, she isn't one of them. Because of her status as a princess, she has seen many men who want her for reasons besides just her. Even though she knows that Albin's affections for her are true, she knows that is not the case with Gavin.

Putting two and two together, she is sure that he must have an ulterior motive for helping Albin besides being thankful. After all, she recognizes the fact that this hopeless romantic is a valuable member of the chief's council.

Interrupting his thought, Nimue says, "Well, I don't trust him. You were going to say that you suspect him, weren't you?"

"The thought has crossed my mind, but I cannot publicly point him out without any evidence," Albin admits.

"Are you serious? If you suspect him, why are we just standing here idle? If he is willing to kill one of his own, what makes you think he is going to stand by quietly? For all we know, he is planning on killing every one of us slowly. Are you actually going to allow him to kill again just because you don't have any *evidence*?"

Looking sheepish, Albin doesn't know what to say.

Then, she says, "What if his next target is the chief? What if it's me?"

That certainly gets his attention.

"What do you want me to do?" Albin asks with a troubled look in his eyes.

"I want you to tail him and find out what he is up to, of course!"

"Of course, princess. I will do as you commend."

"And, I need you to help me get the morale of our people back up. They are all so scared of what is happening that they are losing their minds. I am afraid to see what they will do if they start to lose control."

"What do you suggest?"

"Come on, walk with me," Nimue says as she looks around.

Being the suspicious type, she always thinks that there is a spy lurking in the shadows, just listening in. Hence, she never discusses important strategies in the same location for an extended amount of time. She figures it's harder for the spies to keep up if she is always on the move. After Albin's little eavesdropping incident at the chief's hut, she doesn't even trust that location to be secure anymore. Of course, she is right to be a little paranoid.

During this entire conversation, Fouke is listening in, but doesn't care. He has always known that the princess does not trust him. So far, she has not done a very good job. Telling Albin to do the same is not going to change anything, considering that he is just a weak pushover. As far as he is concerned, he is winning this war. Before long, the island will be in such chaos that he can easily take over without any resistance.

"Who needs Balavan, anyways?" Fouke mutters to himself before going back to Nonni and Grami's hut.

196

After listening to the trial and to Numei's conversation with Albin, he is more than confident that he has nothing to worry about.

As he enters the hut, Grami asks, "Where have you been Gavin? I have been looking for you?"

Just as he has planned, he has an excuse.

"I was at the trial."

"I thought you didn't want to be there," Grami asks with a suspicious eye.

"I didn't, but I just couldn't stay away. I want to know what kind of monster can kill a friend."

Seemingly satisfied with the answer, Grami says, "Please go hunt a deer for me. I want to prepare a feast for the neighbors to brighten their day a little. They all seem to be quite depressed by recent events."

"Certainly," Fouke replies as a dutiful servant, all the while smiling and thinking that everything is working exactly as he has hoped.

*

In the meantime, Thom is on his way to Trozos with his team of eager men who are determined to capture Fouke – dead or alive. With Torgny's directions in hand, they take off for their mission at dusk so they can land on the island in the middle of the night to avoid detection. As they navigate their way through the rough waters, however, they can hear debris hitting the side of their boat as the waves lap against it. Taking out a strobe light, Thom and his crew see the remnants of a boat.

"What do you think?" Valentine asks.

"About what?" Thom replies without giving it a second thought.

As far as Thom is concerned, it can be from anywhere and could have come from the other side of the planet and has been floating for months, maybe even years. He is no expert at these things and has no intention of being one. All he cares about is battle tactics and weaponry. Valentine, however, is the exact opposite. As a former scout and current intelligence officer, there is no detail too small to be ignored. From what he sees, there seems to be a great deal of evidence in the water that is concerning.

"About the destroyed vessel."

"What of it?"

"Whose do you think it is?"

Judging from the material and the marking on the debris, Valentine is pretty sure that it had come from Balavan. Not having seen it before its departure, however, he is not aware that this boat once belonged to Russell's crew. It is the same one that Chief Cai had destroyed, no, *demolished*, to ward off anyone else who may try to come on his island. The chief's men really outdid themselves. It is not just in pieces, but mangled with nails bent in every direction. They even put some pig's blood on the planks before letting them loose in the water.

"I don't know. It can be anybody," Thom says nonchalantly.

Fishing a piece of wood out of the water, Valentine studies it closely. In addition to putting his face level to it to look at every grain and stain, he feels its texture and smells the scent.

Then, he concludes, "I am almost positive that this is fresh wreckage from Balavan. The only people I know of who left our dominion in recent days are Russell and his crew."

Upon hearing his explanation, Thom is interested. If Russell's men are dead, it makes his job that much easier.

"Think any of them are still alive?"

Touching the grain again, he says, "Possibly, but I cannot be sure."

Dismayed, Thom points at the rubbles and asks, "Look at it! How can any of them survive something like that? There is not a single sustainable piece of the craft left."

"The damage is not caused by nature. It looks like this vessel was hacked into pieces by someone. Hence, they either encountered an enemy at sea or on shore. My bet is on shore. It would be very difficult for someone to do this kind of damage on top of turbulent water. If they were defeated on land, there is a possibility that they are being held prisoner for one reason or another."

Thom is quite intrigued. He has not thought of that possibility. That means the natives on Trozos Island are more bloodthirsty than he had expected. He is also starting to wonder if this is all one big trap, not just for him, but for Russell, too. Even though he was the one who volunteered for the mission, he cannot help but think that Violet knew about the risks and intentionally allowed him to walk to his death. Yet, he is more excited than anything else.

"Oh, well, even if she did, I don't blame her," Thom says to himself as he shrugs it off.

Thom has never been one to be afraid of anything. That is another reason that he offered to go on this voyage. Sitting around just going through the motions of training is starting to suck the life out of him, adding to his already depressed state. He has to face a certain level of danger to feel alive again. This seems to be the perfect opportunity.

Being elite members of the Desiderios, Thom figures everyone else feels the same and thinks nothing of it.

"Well, let's make sure that everyone is ready for a fight then," Thom responses calmly.

Nodding, Valentine informs the rest of the crew of their conclusions. Instantly, everyone is busy sharpening their blades and cleaning their firearms to make sure that everything is in tip top shape. If Torgny had planned for the Desiderios to go quietly, he will certainly be disappointed. At this point, Thom doesn't really care what the elderly spy has planned. All he knows is that there is no turning back now.

*

At the same time, Russell is pondering what he should do. He is going over the previous day's event over and over again, trying to think of something, anything that can help him vindicate his friend. All he can think of are a bunch of laughter and a sense of euphoria that he has never felt before, but that information is completely useless. None of that is going to help his friend.

"This will not do!" Russell chastises himself.

He needs to do more than think. Judging from the looks of things, the trial is going to continue exactly the same way as it has been for the last three hours. Poor Cameron's answers are exactly the same no matter how the guard captain rephrases the questions. The only difference is the volume of his voice. It is getting lower with each word. There is no point staying there any longer. It is getting almost too painful to watch. Instead, he needs different scenery to try to jot his memory.

As he starts to walk away from the trial, he finds himself going back to the scene of the crime without realizing it. As he walks into the room, he shivers as a sense of dread and misery surrounds him instantly. He looks around. Everything is exactly as they left it. The bed sheet is still in the state of upheaval. The blood stain is still on the ground. The bath water is still in the tub along with the rose petals and the scented oil that the ladies have poured in it. Yet, everything looks so different now. The petals are wilted and the water is murky and cold. The water spilled on the once clean and shiny wooden floor has now dried into brown and crusty stains.

Pacing the room back and forth, he has no idea what he is looking for. Despite being a strategist, he has never had to use that talent as an investigator before. He is not sure where to start. Even though he is looking at every detail of the room, he is not actually seeing anything. It's as if his brain is not working even though his eyes are. Hitting the side of his head, he tries to concentrate, as if beating himself makes any difference.

"Think! Stupid! Think!" he says to himself.

Taking a deep breath, he continues to mumble to himself, "I was over there. Owen was there. Cameron was here. The door is over there."

Putting his face on the ground, he is looking to see if there are any traces of blood going to the door to support his theory that an intruder was the murderer. Getting up, he shakes his head. There are a lot of foot prints on the floor. When the ladies walked in, they walked on the blood and left little prints behind. When the guards came in to arrest Cameron, they also stepped on some of the blood, leaving the larger footprints.

"Wait, where did they take Owen's body?" he wonders.

After all of this chaos, he has not thought about his brother's corpse. He has to bring him back to Balavan for a proper burial. As he walks towards the spot where his brother's body lied, he looks at the pool of blood and the foot prints immediately surrounding his body. Suddenly, he notices something.

Owen had been lying in the corner of the hut, where there was a thicker layer of dirt than the rest of the hut. On the side opposite of the other footprints, there was a slight indent in the floor where two footprints were made.

While the rest of the footprints had been made on top of the blood, these were clean. Even though there was blood spatter on the wall on that side, there was no blood spatter on the ground, like someone had been there and gotten splattered instead. He leaned closer, staring at the indent, it was a clear and definite footprint, like the guards and ladies had never stepped over the footprints.

While the prints made by the ladies all look the same because they all wear the same type of shoes with similarly small feet, the guards also are required to wear the same types of shoes. There is a third set of shoe prints that are made by someone else. Because neither he nor Cameron stepped that close to the body when they woke up, neither of them could have made those. Besides, they were both barefoot when the guards came to take Cameron away.

"That must be the murderer's!" Russell says to himself as he starts to get excited.

With this realization, it seems his head has also become clear all of a sudden. Immediately, he starts to take detailed pictures of the footprints. He is actually surprised that he hadn't thought about photographing the scene of the crime yet. Isn't that what every detective does first when they find a dead body?

As he keeps staring at the prints, he makes another startling conclusion. This print is made by a pair of military boots. It had a distinct pattern that only military made boots would have. Stepping back, he is in shock. None of the islanders wear boots, let alone military ones. They all wear soft moccasins that cannot possibly make such deep grooved prints. There is only one person on this island he can think of who may wear that type of footwear – Fouke.

While Fouke changed his clothes to that of the natives, he never bothered to get a different pair of shoes. In order to go from one part of the island to another on a daily bases, he needs a good, sturdy pair of shoes. The moccasins that the locals wear are just not durable enough for the task. It's also not fast enough when he needs to be on the run and does not have enough grip if he needs to climb trees or rooftops. Hence, even though he owns a pair, he only wears them when he is trying to blend in with the neighbors. He normally does not wear it when he is out and about.

On the day of the murder, he needed his boots. Being very confident with himself, he never bothered to get rid of the prints before leaving the scene of the crime. Besides, he figures these people are too backward to check for things like that. He also figures that Russell is too inexperienced to know what to look for in times of an emergency since, in his eyes, he is nothing but a trainee.

"What to do? What to do?" Russell asks himself in frustration.

Now that he has a suspect in mind, he knows he must follow that lead. Knowing Fouke's reputation, he also knows that he does not have much time to be indecisive – one misstep and he can be next. Then, he remembers Albin's testimony about his knife having been stolen that very day. Even though he doesn't know this Albin, he seems to be a nice man. He is hoping that together, they can help each other solve this mystery. Albin can help him find the man who framed Cameron. In return, he can help his new partner find the man who stole his dagger.

As he walks back down the streets looking for Albin, he has no idea who he is. He does not know about his affection for the princess, his friendship with Fouke, or his position in the chief's council. All he cares is that this is the man who is going to help him get out of a bind. Unfortunately, without Cameron as his translator, looking for Albin is no easy task.

After spotting three teenage boys who are kicking a ball back and forth to one another, he goes up to them and says, "Excuse me, can you tell me where Albin lives?"

Not knowing his language, the boys look at each other with a puzzled look.

In their native tongue, one boy says, "What did he say?"

Another responds, "I don't know, but I think he mentioned Albin."

Hearing the name repeated, Russell says, "Yes, yes, Albin. Can you help me find him?"

The first boy says, "There it is again. He said his name. What do you think he wants?"

The third boy looks Russell in the eyes and slowly shouts, "Are you looking for Albin?"

Russell always wonders why people shout and enunciate words slowly when they are speaking a different language. He's not deaf. Besides, it's not like he is going to understand it any better if he doesn't know it at all in the first place. Nevertheless, knowing that the boy is shouting Albin's name means that he seems to understand what he is saying. Realizing that answering in his own language is completely useless, he simply nods. It's probably a lot easier to use sign language to speak with these boys than actual speech.

The second boy says, "Come on, follow us."

204

As the boys pick up their ball and run towards Albin's hut, Russell follows closely by. Seeing how an outsider is running through their island, many of the locals take notice as they mumble to each other again.

"What is that idiot doing running so fast? Is he chasing the boys?" one woman asks her husband.

Another woman shouts, "Close your doors! The outsider is running amuck!"

With those words of caution, many of the islanders grab their children in fear again. Russell knows perfectively well that his welcome is going to come to an end very quickly. If he does not solve this mystery, he is afraid that these seemingly peaceful islanders may take matters into their own hands soon.

Then, the boys stop in front of a hut as the first boy shouts, "Here it is!"

Russell says, "Thank you," as he bows to the boys.

Then, reaching into his pocket, he takes out loose change and gives the boys a couple of coins. The boys are all so delighted. They have never seen these coins before. Even though it has very little monetary value, they are all giddy with joy as they compare each one with one another.

"Thank you, mister!" the third boy shouts as they happily go back to where he found them.

Some of the onlookers who have being gawking at Russell actually have a smile on their faces when they see how happy the boys are. Maybe, the outsiders are not so bad after all.

Knocking on the door, Russell says, "Hello? Anybody home?"

After not getting a response, he opens the door slowly and says, "I am Russell. I am wondering if I may have a word with you. Hello?"

Disappointed, Russell has hoped to find him there, but the hut appears to be empty. Sitting down at the kitchen table, he suddenly realizes that he smells something familiar. Even though the windows are open, there is still a trace of the aroma from Fouke's cooking left in the air. Sniff, sniff, Russell recognizes that scent anywhere. It's one of his favorite dishes back home. Walking towards the kitchen, he sees the dirty dishes still in the sink. Looking at the crumbs left on the plates, he is sure of it, but just to be doubly sure, he puts his pinky on the plate and takes a taste.

"Yep, that's it!" Russell says to himself.

Now, there is no doubt that the person who killed Owen has been in Albin's hut that day and he is from Balavan. After taking pictures of the plate, he walks around to see if he can find anything useful there. As he opens cabinets, it doesn't take him long to find the vial that Fouke has given Albin. Taking it out, it takes a sniff. He knows exactly what it is, but just like Albin, he does not know that it is poisoned. All he knows is that the same person who cooked the dish must have left it there, which makes him wonder if Fouke is living in that hut.

Then, a disturbing thought comes to mind. Is Albin partnering up with Fouke to kill Owen and frame Cameron? He doesn't want to believe it, but it is a definitely possibility. After all, Torgny has said that the islanders do not like outsiders and want them out. Perhaps, Albin has teamed up with Fouke in order to get rid of them, not realizing that Fouke is more dangerous than he appears. That can explain why Albin wouldn't give up the name of the suspect. Perhaps, the dagger was not stolen. What if he had willingly given it to Fouke? He shudders at the thought. If that is the case, there is no point hanging around. He is not going to help him. In fact, he may even find ways to sabotage him. Once again, he is at the crossroads and doesn't know what to do.

Chapter 16: The Attack

While Fouke is enjoying himself, he is completely unaware of Thom's imminent arrival. Although he is fully aware that if Russell has found his way to Trozos Island, someone from the Desiderios is not far behind, he is not worried at this point. Considering that he has been on this island for so long, he has an edge over them. He knows the people better and has built a positive reputation with most of them. He also has hidden weapons that only he can access. Hence, when they do show up, he is ready for them. At least, that is what he is telling himself.

The same cannot be said of the islanders. While they are visibly shaken by recent events, they are not anywhere near ready to battle a formidable force like the Desideros, even though there are only a few dozen of them. Relying on their daunting reputation, the islanders have been able to get away with playing tough rather than actually being tough. They don't even have modern weapons like guns or cannons. They also do not have modern communication system.

Instead, relying on face to face meetings and written reports. While this may seem archaic to the outside world, this works for them because it makes sure that none of their secrets can be leaked out accidentally. At the same time, this also means that they have no way of getting backup quickly.

By nightfall, the trial is finally over, even though they have not gotten any closer to finding the real culprit. At the same time, they are not willing to let their only suspect go just yet. Despite being fairly certain that he is telling the truth, the chief cannot overlook the fact that he has the murder weapon in his hand when he was caught. Locking Cameron back to the makeshift prison hut, the guards have returned to their respective homes for the day. Besides the tension that is still lingering in the air, most of the people seem to have returned back to their normal lives. With Cameron out of sight, they have opened their windows back up as the cool breeze once again flows through their homes.

Despite the seemingly calm sea, the tranquility is just an illusion that is not going to last for long. As they all begin to turn in for the night, Thom is getting closer to the island. He can see it already with his naked eyes and is more than ready for this fight. Instead of bearing gifts, he is carrying heavy weaponry. Instead of being on a peaceful journey to bring Fouke home, he is on a destructive one to bring the Major back to face justice.

Turning off all sources of light and shutting off their engines, they coast slowly to shore. Ironically, arriving in the dark of the night is not nearly as scary as coming ashore during the day. Despite the flickering of the torches, it is difficult to see the macabre skeletons that line the beaches. Without being able to see the details, it actually looks quite pretty – almost like a tropical resort of some sort.

*

Being in an empty hut some distance from the rest of the village, Cameron can hear every sound in the surrounding areas from the crickets and the frogs to the muted chattering of the locals in their homes and the palm leaves rustling in the wind. Even though there are two windows in his tiny holding cell, they are small and too high up on the walls for him to be able to look outside. Since the hut was originally designed to be a storage shed, the windows serve only as ventilation, which is just as well.

Now that he is alone, he can let out his frustrations in his own way. Sitting in the corner with nothing but a sandwich, a glass of water, and a small pot for him to do his business, tears are flowing through the corner of his eyes, wondering how he is going to get out of this mess. He hoped that Russell would come to his rescue, but he is deeply disappointed that he has not seen him since his arrest. Even though Russell was in the trial, he stayed at a distance and has not tried to contact him, not because he doesn't care, but because he needs to come up with a plan first. There is no point in being implicated and arrested along with Cameron if he intends on saving him.

As he tries to distract his mind from the days' events and his impending doom, he focuses his hearing to the gentle sound of the sea lapping onto the shore. Then, suddenly, his ears perk up. Even though it is faint, he hears something *different*. He knows that sound is not from the coconuts hitting the ground or from the animals wandering through the trees. The low scraping crashes that knock against the rocks distinctively sound human made and big. He tries to jump up to see if he can look out the window, but he just barely misses the opening. Without a chair or table to stand on, he can only hang on the window. Even if he does manage to lift himself up enough, there is not enough room on the ceiling for him.

Realizing that they may be in dire danger, he shouts as loud as he can. "Hey, is there anybody out there?"

After a few seconds of silence, he shouts louder, thinking that he is too far away to be heard even though the relative silence from the rest of the island should make it easier.

"Hello? Anybody?"

Hearing his faint shouts, the locals ignore him. Even though he seemed like a timid man during the trial, they think he is just trying to get attention so he can get away. Either that or he is simply going out of his mind after being grilled for so many hours in a humiliating cage.

While he tries to listen for people coming his way, he hears the sound of the mysterious intruder's boat coming closer instead. Not knowing the identity of the newcomers, he has no idea if it's friend or foe. On the other hand, no friend that he knows of ever comes to visit a remote island in the middle of the night, especially not one that arrives in what sounds like a very large boat.

Frustrated and anxious at the same time, he finally says, "Somebody! I think the island is about to be attacked! Wake up!"

That seems to have gotten some of the locals' attention. Even though Cameron cannot see anyone, he does see lights coming on from different direction. At least, some of the people are looking to see if there is something going on even if they are not answering him. Then, he hears the murmuring of the people getting louder and louder.

It seems he is right. The island is being attacked.

Before long, he hears footsteps running in every direction as he hears some people crying. At the same time, he hears people hushing one another. As he is wondering what is happening outside, he hear someone right outside of his hut. Then, he hears the sound he has been hoping to hear – click.

A man that looked like one of the guards comes in and shouts, "Come on, let's go!"

It is the sweetest voice he has ever heard, not because of the quality of the sound or the way it was spoken. It is because of the person who said it. Even though it is too dim in the hut to be able to see the identity of his rescue, he immediately recognizes the voice.

It is Russell. He has finally come through for him. Even though he doubted him earlier in the night, his faith in his friend has been completely restored. Even in that moment of chaos, he feels guilty for having not believed in him.

210

With a spear in hand, Russell hands Cameron a dagger before running into the woods. With the panic all around the island, no one even notices that they have escaped.

Once they are completely out of sight, Cameron gives his friend a big hug and says, "Thank you! Thank you! Thank you! How can I ever repay you?"

"Don't thank me yet. We are still way over our heads."

"I don't know who is coming onshore at this time of the hour, but I am sure glad they did!" Cameron says joyously.

"Shhh! I don't think we should be celebrating. I don't think these are friends. We need to find out who it is. I didn't tell anyone where we were going or the location of this island before we left, except Iris. I don't think that's her. That means that these people are not part of our group. That would leave the Desiderios.

If El Diablo or the Warrior is leading the attack, Trozos is as good as gone. In either case, we need to find our boat and leave immediately before we get caught in the middle of all this."

As they walk to the other side of the island where they landed, they are shocked that it is nowhere to be found. The chief's men did such a good job of scattering the pieces into the sea that there is not a single trace of it left. Scratching their heads, the both wonder if the tide has taken their craft somewhere else. Going to higher ground, they search for any traces of their boat. When they get to the top of a hill, all they see are the islanders lighting torches and gathering on shore as the mysterious boat anchors.

As they are about to descend back to the village, cannon balls are fired, sending the villagers into shear panic as they scream and run for cover. Shocked, Cameron and Russell look at each other.

"What in the world?!? Why are they firing at the villagers?" Russell says in disbelief.

Without binoculars, neither one of them can see what is really going on down there. Everyone looks like tiny ants squirming around aimlessly in the dark with speckles of torches like fireflies. Then, they see small sparks that look like gun shots lighting up the starry night as loud popping sounds ring out the entire island amidst the sounds of gut wrenching cries. Hiding on the hill top, neither one of them wants to move from their safe hiding place.

"Who do you think is attacking the island?" Cameron asks as he shivers.

"I don't know. Whoever they are sure are relentless," Russell laments.

"What should we do now?"

"Nothing. We need to wait until the fire fight is over before we see which side has won."

"Isn't it obvious? The villagers are being slaughtered down there!"

"True," Russell says.

Even though he knows about El Diablo's reputation for looking death in the eyes, he has never thought of him as a cold blooded murderer. Even though he cannot think of anyone besides the Desiderios who may be down there, he just cannot imagine them launching an attack like this. Despite being put on trial for a murder he did not commit, Cameron is starting to feel sorry for the islanders.

"I think we should go down there and help them."

"How?" Russell asks as he looks completely helpless.

It seems the leader has become the follower. He has no clue how to help those people without being killed alongside them.

"Come on, let's go!" Cameron says as he starts running towards the village.

"Wait, what's our plan?" Russell shouts behind him.

"This is a really bad idea," he mumbles to himself as he tries to catch up to his friend.

With no weapon and no plans, he is sure that they are running towards their own deaths. What good are two dead men to these villagers? Regardless of how hopeless it looks, however, Russell cannot let Cameron do it on his own. After losing Owen already, he is not about to lose another member of his team, no matter how bad the situation gets.

*

Within seconds of the cannon firing, Fouke is already on his feet. Being a cautious man, he has never been a heavy sleeper. Even though the heavy artillery is a good distance away from Nonni and Grami's hut, he recognizes the sound anywhere.

Like Russell and Cameron, he has no idea who may be attacking the island. Unlike those two, he doesn't really care as long as they are attacking the islanders and not him. Self-preservation is his primary goal right now. Instantly, he gets out of bed as quietly as he can and goes for his secret stash. He has to arm himself in case he gets attacked.

"Where are you going?" Nonni asks.

Surprised, Fouke turns around to see the old lady already dressed. He is sure that these two senior citizens would have slept through the muted sounds of gunfire. For the past few months that he has spent with them, they have never gotten up in the middle of the night before. Then again, they may simply have kept quiet. Besides, he has no one else to compare it to. He has never spent a great deal of time with other elderlies before.

Pretending not to know what that sound is, he looks scared and puzzled as he says, "Do you hear that?"

"Hear what?"

"That sound? It sounds like fireworks."

"It does, doesn't it?" Nonni replies with a serious look on her face.

Alarmed by her expression, Fouke wonders if it's his imagination. It's as if she is testing him and waiting for him to fess up about something. Can the old lady be on to him? That's simply not possible. She has always looked so clueless and almost senile at times. Has it all been an act?

It cannot be. He has always been able to see through anyone who has tried to pull a fast one on him before. How is she any different? Perhaps, he has been too quick to discount her because of her frail appearance. As he ponders how to respond to her, he is unaware that his problems are about to get worse. Within a minute, Grami comes in with his chest of hidden loot.

"Is this yours?" Grami asks, knowing full well that it is.

Now, there is no doubt. He has been caught. These two old ladies are not just there to keep him busy. They have been watching his every move. That means they probably know that he was the one who killed Owen and framed Cameron. If so, they certainly have let the game continue for quite a while. After all, they even let the chief go through the trouble of conducting a public daylong trial. For them to reveal themselves now means that he is in serious trouble. Fouke does the only thing he knows to do in a situation like this – lie.

"I have never seen it before in my life," he replies with his best impression of a deer caught in the headlight.

Playing along, Grami tries to provoke him and says, "Hm, I wonder who would bury such things near our home. Most people on the island have no problem just leaving their things out in the open. The owner of this chest must not be very trusting."

Pretending not to know what the objects are, Nonni and Grami study them, polish them with their shirts, and put them in their own pockets, as they continue to try to get a rise out of their guest. So far, he is not taking the bait. With the sound of the battle raging on, Fouke knows that his time is running out. If he doesn't get away from them soon, he is a sitting duck. From the sound of it, the intruders don't play around. If they have no problem blasting away at innocent villagers, they certainly will not blind twice shooting at their intended target. Hence, if they are here for him, he is as good as dead if he doesn't move quickly.

Trying to make light of the situation, Fouke shrugs and says, "Your guess is as good as mine!"

Taking out the longest sword, Grami says, "Well, this man does not appear to be very friendly."

Getting impatient, Fouke changes the subject and says, "I am going to go check out the fireworks. Don't wait up!"

As he heads towards the door, Nonni says, "Where do you think you are going?"

"I just told you. I am going to see the fireworks."

"I don't think so."

Sensing that there is no point continuing the little charade, he smirks and coldly says, "Who's going to stop me?"

As he continues to walk, Nonni jumps in front of him with one of his own swords pointed right on his throat as she twists his right arm behind him and says, "We are."

Panicking, Fouke has obviously underestimated these two old ladies. He has always thought of them as nothing more than a babysitter, too old to be able to defend themselves if he tries anything. He figures the worst they can do is hightail back to the chief and tell on him. He has never been so wrong. These two women are much more agile than they had him think. Despite being proud of his ability to sniff out a con, he has definitely been had.

As Grami quickly ties his hands behind his back, she says, "Who is attacking us?"

"I don't know," Fouke says.

Even though he is telling the truth, it's too late for that. Neither Nonni nor Grami believe his act of innocence anymore.

Nicking his neck with the sword, Nonni says, "Do you think we are joking?"

"No, no, please! I really don't know!"

"Who have you been contacting? First, that Russell and his team of buffoons show up. Now, these ruthless bandits are attacking us. I am warning you. If you don't tell us what we need to know in the next minute, you will lose a body part."

"I swear I don't know who they are!" Fouke protests as he struggles to get loose.

"That is not going to cut it," Grami says as she cuts his left cheek, pun intended.

"Ouch! Please stop! I am not lying!"

"Oh, like you are not lying about your identity, *Gavin*?"

Knowing that there is no point lying, he says, "OK, my *real* name is Brandon Fouke. I was a Major for the Legionnaires in Balavan. When we lost, I became a wanted criminal. That is the only reason I lied about who I am. But, that is all I lied about. I swear!"

"Oh, really, and how do you explain the death of this Owen fellow?"

"I cannot!" Fouke exclaims, still hoping that he can get away with *something*.

Cutting his other cheek, Grami says, "I know you killed him."

His worst fear has been realized. His cover is completely blown.

"If you already know all of that, why are you still asking?"

Getting into his face, Grami says, "Still trying to be cheeky, huh?"

Again, pun is intended. After all, she seems to enjoy cutting his cheeks every time he gives a less than satisfactory answer.

"No! I am not! I really don't know who these people are. I can guess, but that is all I can do. I really don't know who they are! I haven't heard anything about an attack. I can tell you who I guess they may be, but it's purely a guess."

Since he is repeating himself in the same breath, Nonni figures he is probably telling the truth.

"Fine, humor us. Who do you *guess* these attackers are?"

Taking a sigh of relief, Fouke says, "I think they are members of the Desiderios, the people who have been hunting me."

"Then, why are they attacking the villagers?"

"Well, their leader's name is El Diablo. So, what do you think?"

Cutting him again, Grami says, "What I think is I should just kill you right now since you are being less than helpful."

This time the cut is deep enough for blood to be dripping constantly. Fouke knows that joke time is over. She is losing her patience and getting more aggressive. He needs to keep her in check before she makes good on her promise to detach a body part. He shudders to think which part she has in mind.

"OK, OK, I am sorry! I don't know why they are attacking the villagers exactly, but my best guess is that someone must have given them a reason to be on the defensive. Perhaps, someone gave them a warning shot before they landed that made them think that the islanders are hostile."

"*Defensive*? So, are you saying that they are not the kind that kills unless they are provoked?"

"I wouldn't put it that way, but, yes. They are generally the cautious type. They don't usually go on an offensive unless they have a good reason."

"So, you are saying that somebody told them to attack us," Nonni says.

Now, her face becomes a little ashen. What he said must have hit a nerve. Fouke wonders what that means.

Composing herself, Nonni says, "Let's go."

"Where are we going?" Fouke protests.

"That's for you to find out," Nonni replies without slowing down.

*

Down in the village, it is complete and total chaos. While Chief Cai and his guards are in full force and have

218

been trying to fight back the hostile invasion, Nimue and Albin are doing their best to help the villagers. Neither of them are having too much luck. With each child saved, two are being injured. Without modern weaponry, Chief Cai's men are no match for Thom. After realizing that there is no point continuing this losing battle, Chief Cai makes a very painful decision.

With an anguished look on his face, he says, "Do it."

"Are you sure, Sire?" his guard captain replies hesitantly.

Nodding, he confirms his unspoken order. He has to accept defeat in hopes of saving the lives of the remaining islanders. It is entirely his fault for not preparing for this battle. He has seen it coming, but has underestimated the tenacity of his enemies. Having lived in relative peace for so long, he has lost his edge and it's time for him to pay the price. Turning on a bright flood light, the captain of the guards put up the white flag of surrender.

Chapter 17: The Guilt

The light is so bright that it catches the attention of everyone on the island, including Thom's men. Seeing the flag of truce, Thom orders his men to cease fire. Almost instantly, all fighting stops, not a moment too soon. Putting their hands up in the air, Chief Cai, Princess Nimue, and his guard captain walk towards Thom's boat, ready to accept whatever form of punishment the invaders have in mind.

Getting off the boat with his men, Thom smiles as he walks up to the chief triumphantly. He, too, is glad that the fighting is over. Despite his experience as a general for the Legionnaires, there is only so much carnage he can stomach. He is still a gentleman, after all.

With Princess Nimue translating, Chief Cai holds out his ceremonial staff and says, "I am Chief Cai of the Trozians. I accept our defeat. Please do as you wish with me, but please spare my people."

Laughing, Thom accepts the staff and replies, "Thanks, but I am no barbarian."

Somewhat relieved that Thom seems to be quite laid back despite the destruction that his men have incurred on his island, the chief asks, "If you don't mind my asking, may I ask the name of our conqueror?"

"Oh, where are my manners? I am Thomas Richardson of the Desiderios."

Upon hearing his name, Chief Cai is a little intimidated by his reputation, but keeps it to himself and asks, "Pray tell, why have you come to attack us?"

Seeing that there is no harm telling the chief what happened, Thom tells him about his discovery of the remnants of Russell's boat.

Realizing that his plans have backfired, the chief is ashamed as he asks, "I don't understand. Why would you attack us simply because of wreckage?"

Referring to their cannibalistic reputation, Thom says, "From the looks of the wreckage, I thought for sure you fellows are ruthless barbarians who have eaten Russell and his men. I figure you would have captured and cooked us, too, if we didn't take charge first. I see I was wrong."

A little insulted and a little embarrassed, the chief says, "What brings you to our island?"

Raising his voice so that the villagers can hear him, Thom shouts, "I am on a hunt for a man named Major Brandon Fouke. I believe he has landed here several months ago. I intend to bring him home to face justice for war crimes."

By now, dawn is approaching. For the first time since the beginning of their nightmare, everyone on the island, Russell and Cameron included, are able to get a glimpse of the invaders who have attacked them. Considering that they have suffered such a great loss, no one can blame the villagers for not caring what Thom has to say. Those who are unharmed are mumbling to each other while those who are injured are groaning in agony.

After seeing Thom with his own eyes, Russell turns ashen as he instantly grabs Cameron by the shirt to stop him from continuing his charge towards the village. It's best to lay low to avoid being detected in a time like this. When Cameron was merely a wrongfully accused fugitive on a deserted island full of trusting people, Russell didn't find a need to stop him. Somehow, he figures running down to the village would be seen as bravery rather than stupidity in the eyes of the villagers.

But, that is not the case with Thom. After all, the Desiderios are not exactly their friends. He wound hate to be implicated for something else that neither one of them have done. Not that he thinks Thom would falsely accuse anyone of any wrong doing, but he wants to be on the safe side. After the roller coaster ride he has been on since he embarked on this journey, nothing can surprise him now.

Not wanting to prolong the inevitable and risk inciting Thom any further, the chief says, "We have the man you want."

"Excellent! Where is he?"

Seeing the chief nod at him, he guard captain says, "Yes, Sire."

As he and another guard head towards Nonni and Grami's hut as quickly as they can, they see the two old ladies coming towards them with Fouke.

"Sorry to keep you waiting. Here is the man you are looking for," Nonni announces.

Seeing Fouke's hands tied up like that being led by two feeble looking elderly women makes Thom laugh.

"This is rich!" Thom says. "I didn't realize that all it takes to capture this man is two old ladies! I cannot believe we have wasted so much time hunting him down!"

As the guards meet up with them, they take over the prisoner. When they get back to Thom, they throw him to the ground. It's quite a sight. The once proud Major Fouke is now speechless on his knees as his head hangs low. It's definitely not something that Thom has expected to see before he embarked on this journey. What happened to the once proud and cocky major?

This is but of a shadow of the man he once knew. Even when Thom was his commanding officer, he never saw him bend over for anyone before, let alone bowed down like this in front of everyone. Fouke has never accepted defeat of any kind. What changed? He almost feels sorry for this man.

222

"Wait," Thom chastises to himself.

This must be just another one of his infamous tactics. Fouke knows that he has been caught and there is no way of escaping. The only way he can get out of this is to get his captors to have sympathy for him and give him leniency. That is exactly what he is feeling. Thom is not about to fall for one of his tricks again. He has seen enough of it.

"Oh, no, he is not getting me with that one," Thom thinks to himself.

Nevertheless, Nooni can sense that slight bit of hesitation and she is not about to give Fouke any chance of getting off the hook after the havoc that he has caused.

Stepping up to the chief who is still standing next to Thom, she says, "Sire, if you please, we have urgent news to report regarding the prisoner."

Knowing that she is really saying it to both of them, the chief nods and says, "Go on."

Taking out the buried chest, Grami opens it and says, "These are the things that he has been collecting over the past few months."

She doesn't need to elaborate. The loot speaks for itself. Looking at the weapons and the tools, they both know what that means. Fouke has been planning an attack and is waiting for the opportune moment to launch it. The chief shudders to think what would have happened if he succeeded, especially after Thom has done his damage.

"There is more," Grami says loudly.

The villagers have never heard either Nonni or Grami speak so much or so loudly before. It's like they are completely different people than the old ladies that they thought they know. Despite the destruction that is still surrounding them, many of them turn to listen to what they have to say.

223

Nonni announces, "We have witnessed with our own eyes that this man is also the one who murdered the outsider."

With this damaging testimony, there is a loud uniform gasp coming from the village before they start to mumble with each other. After they have everyone's attention, they recount the events that they saw that fateful day starting with the moment that Fouke stole the dagger from Albin's hut to the instant that he planted it in Cameron's hand. As Fouke expected, these two have been spying on him. Now, the entire island knows. Even the chief looks a little surprised by what he has heard. The one who is the most surprised, however, is Cameron.

"Did... Did you hear what I think I heard?" Cameron says with wide eyes.

Nodding, Russell smiles and pats his friend on the shoulder and says, "He confessed."

Cameron is so happy that tears are coming out of the corner of his eyes without him realizing it. Ordinarily, Russell would have told him to hide his emotions. After all, they are supposed to be proud soldiers. But, today, he figures he will let him have his moment. It's not every day that one gets to be exonerated for a crime he didn't commit. Of course, while Cameron's troubles are over, Fouke's has just started.

"What do you have to say in your defense?" the chief asks.

Fouke simply kneels there silently. He has no idea how to get out of this one. All he can think of is how he made the mistake of underestimating these two women. Looking at Thom, the Chief looks to see if he has anything else planned, but he see none. Thom seems to be happy to have captured him in the first place. Anything else is no longer his concern.

Finally, the chief announces, "By your silence, I take that as an admission of guilt. For the crime of murder, I sentence you to death."

By now, Fouke is so numb that he no longer feels or hears anything. He also no longer cares. For the first time in his life, he has given up. It looks to be the only time.

That night at 6PM, the chief orders his execution.

Before the axe falls on his head, the chief says one last time, "Do you have anything to say before you depart from this world?"

Fouke looked up at him; eyes dim with defeat but shedding no tears. He would never cry in front of these people. He would die, but he would die proudly, so for a second he thought. Then he says, "Have you ever wondered why we were all sent here in the first place?"

Although those words do resonate in the chief's mind, he doesn't let it bother him before he gives the signal. The ax falls down, ending the proud Major Fouke's life.

*

As Thom stands there savoring his victory, he puts his hands into his pockets for the first time since he embarked on this journey. While there is nothing in either of them, he feels something hard on the inner side, like paper. As he reaches into his inside jacket pocket, he takes out an old piece of paper that has been folded. It's also dingy and wrinkled, as though it'd been through a lot.

Unfolding it, he finds three separate pieces of papers, all of which look like they were written by the same person. The penmanship is definitely feminine, but not one that he immediately recognizes. As he begins to read the first one, he realizes that they are private journal entries.

*

February 28, 2072

What have I gotten myself into? I am so scared! Mom and Dad are going to be SO furious! What should I do? What should I do? I want to keep it, but I don't know if I can. I don't know if I have it in me to do it.

Should I tell him? I don't want him to leave me. I cannot face it if he does. I love him so. I don't want to scare him away, but I am sure he will be able to tell soon. I can feel the bump already.

*

While Thom is not sure what this entry is about exactly, he has a good idea. It sounds like a young girl has gotten herself pregnant and she is scared out of her mind.

"I wonder who she is," Thom asks himself.

There is no name anywhere on the page to give him a hint, but the date looks suspicious. He was born that year. Is this someone he knows, a friend perhaps? It cannot be Max. His parents are not that young. Then, he continues to read the second page. There are several large tear stains smeared on this entry.

*

September 20, 2072

The day has finally come. It's both the happiest day of my life and the saddest one as well. My baby boy is here, but I don't dare to look at him. It's just too painful. If I see how beautiful he is, I am afraid I won't be able to let go. I know I must give him up, but how can I?

Mom and Dad don't know that I am having this baby. They think I am a good girl. I simply cannot disappoint them now. Even though they have wondered why I dressed in such loose clothing for the last nine months, they just thought that I am at a weird stage in my life and am going through an awkward growth spurt. If I come home with the baby, they are surely going to be ashamed of me. I fear they may even throw me out of the house. What would I do then? I cannot let the baby starve. Now that B has left me, I have no one else to turn to.

A nice old couple have asked to take my sweet little boy. Their names are Victor and Amelia Richardson. They say they have a lot of money and have not been able to have a baby of their own. They promise me that they will take care of him like their own and cherish him every day of their lives. But I have to promise to never reveal myself to my baby. I don't know if I can do that, but I know I have to.

*

In that instant, his world seems to have turned upside down again. This may be the biggest shock in his life.

"Is … is this my birth mother?" Thom says to himself as his eyes widen in disbelief.

If so, who is she? It never dawned on him that he was adopted. How can this be? He has blue eyes and brown hair, just like Victor. They are also both tall and slender. There is simply too much resemblance for him not to be related to him, but can it be? Then again, those are very

227

common characteristics. He has seen many people in Balavan with those exact same features. Come to think of it, there are many subtle differences between him and the Richardsons.

He never had the same personalities or habits as his parents. Thom had always thought that it just meant that he didn't pick up anything from them because they weren't around much. He didn't have the same body structure of either of his parents as well.

The one thing that also was weird was that he never saw any pictures of his birth. There was no umbilical cord or sonogram of him. He just thought Amelia never liked showing pictures of her when she was pregnant.

Nevertheless, there are enough similarities that no one has ever doubted their relationship. He has always discounted the differences to age or that the characteristics skipped generations. After all, he has no idea what his grandparents look like. Without other living relatives visiting them, he has nothing to compare to. In any case, perhaps, that is why the Richardsons picked him at the hospital. They wanted a baby who they can pass as their own without question.

Turning the pages back and forth, he is hoping to find a signature or initials of some kind to tell him who the journal entries belong to. If these pages magically appear in his possession, somebody must want him to know. Maybe, it's his birth mother. After looking at every part of the papers, he cannot find any. All he can tell from them is that she was probably still in high school, unwed, and living with her parents. She was madly in love with a man who may not return her affections. Who is this B that she is referring to? If she was so afraid that he would leave her, he is probably quite full of himself. Trying to get more clues, he goes to the third and final page.

*

May 16, 2086

I am so proud of my boy! He has been recruited to the Legionnaires! Now, he gets to be closer to his father! Even if he may never know his true identity, at least they will be together.

Oh, how I miss both of them. I wish things have turned out differently for us, but that would just be selfish talking. At least, they are both happy. I couldn't have hoped for better for them. That is more than what I can say for myself.

B is now a Major for the Legionnaires. A Major, can you believe it? I am so proud of him, too. I wish he knows how proud I am of him even if he wants nothing more to do with me.

*

Dropping the papers on the ground, Thom is completely dumbfounded.

"Major? B? Can it be? Can she be referring to Major Brandon Fouke? Is he, or rather was he, my birth father?" Thom says to himself.

He is now completely beside himself. Looking at Fouke's severed head, he sees blood soaked brown hair and lifeless hazel eyes. Even though the colors are not exactly the same, they look eerily similar to his in a less obvious way. Now that he actually has a chance to study the details carefully, Thom realizes that both he and Fouke have wavy hair and round eyes, both characteristics that are missing from either Victor or Amelia.

Putting his hands on his face, he sits down on the ground. What has he done? Has he done it again? Did he just have his father executed? *Again?* All of this time, he thought he is redeeming his soul, but has he actually been selling it to the devil?

Chapter 18: Homecoming

Returning to Balavan with Fouke's body in a makeshift coffin, Thom is an instant sensation.

"Did you hear? It's finally done! Fouke is dead!" the first man to see Thom's boat docking on the beach shouts as he runs through the streets.

This is the day that Violet has been waiting for. She only wishes that Trip was here to see it firsthand. Excited, she comes out of headquarters to greet him as the hero he has hoped to be since the day he joined the Desiderios.

With a sincere smile, the Warrior shows her soft side as she gives him a big hug and says, "Welcome home."

It's the words that he has longed to hear for months. When news spread that he has finally caught the last of the rebellious Legionnaires, everyone comes out to the streets to get a glimpse of him. They smile and cheer for him for finally bringing peace to the entire Dominion.

Despite his glorious return, Thom has never felt worse. He has always wanted such a warm reception, but not like this. Despite the smile and the fist pump in the air, there is a distinct look of sadness in his eyes. Just like Victor, he knows that Fouke is a degenerate man who the world can live without. But, just like Victor, he was his father. He has to live with the guilt of killing a parent again even though he had not known that little bit of detail until it was too late. As the crowd congratulates him, he feels sicker by the minute. He has to try his hardest not to vomit all over the well-wishers.

Just like Victor, he does not regret catching Fouke, but he regrets not having spent some time with him first. At least with Victor, he grew up in his home and got a chance to know him better. If he were to see Victor face to face today, he wouldn't have anything to say to him. It's different with Fouke. He never got a chance to see the real him. It's strange now. He considered him to be his insubordinate subordinate who never let anyone into his personal life. He has so many unanswered questions that he wished he could have answered for him.

What was he really like in private? Did Fouke know that he was his son? If he did, did he regret never having a father and son relationship with him? Would he have been proud of what he has accomplished? What did he know of him, the real him? Did he regret not being with his birth mother? Speaking of whom, who is his birth mother? Is she still alive? There shouldn't be a reason for her not to be. Somebody who knows about their relationship must have put those journal entries into his pocket. Was it Fouke? It couldn't be. His hands were tied behind his back the entire time he was with him. That means someone must have slipped them into his pocket before he started the journey. He has to find out who she is.

As he makes his way through the streets pondering about this mysterious woman, the sounds of the crowd is fading away. Instead, he is looking into the eyes of every woman who may be his mother's age. As he continues to scan, he catches a glimpse of his other mother, Amelia Richardson, wearing dark sunglasses with a serious expression. She does not look happy in the least bit. Now, she has yet another reason to despise him. It seems all of her hopes have been dashed with the death of Fouke. It's official. He is the worst son in the world and it's eating him alive.

*

After his gut wrenching homecoming celebration, he is finally back home. He cannot bear to talk to anyone else today. He has never been so glad to see his old room – big, dark, and solitary. Even though Victor and Amelia no longer live there, he has left their room exactly the way his mother has left it when she stormed out of their mansion. He isn't sure if its guilt or respect, but he knows that that is *their* room and he has no business being in it. As he buries his face in his pillow trying to drown out his guilt, he hears footsteps.

Alarmed, he draws his side pistol and says, "Who's there?"

After a few seconds of total silence, the sounds of the footsteps get louder.

"I am not going to ask you again," Thom says as he cocks his pistol.

Then, he sees a shadow slowly coming into the light. Although his first instinct is to shoot first and ask questions later, a part of him tells him not to. Perhaps, he is hoping that it's a prowler here to kill him and end his misery. Standing in the open, he waits for the intruder to show himself.

"Hello, Thom," a soft woman's voice says.

Even though he has no idea who she is, she looks familiar. He has seen her before somewhere, but he cannot place it.

"I am at a disadvantage. You know who I am, but I have no idea who you are," he says cautiously as he keeps his gun in his hand even though he has lowered it.

"I am Lenore."

"Is that name supposed to mean something to me?"

"No, I suppose not."

233

"Are you going to tell me why you broke into my home?" Thom says impatiently while he tries to remember where he may have seen her before.

"I want to speak with you – in private."

"Well, you could have done that without committing a felony," he says sarcastically.

"I know, but secrecy is of utmost importance."

"Whatever. What do you want to tell me?"

"Well, first, I want to congratulate you for having captured the most elusive war criminal on the land," Lenore says with a sad look in her eyes.

"Thanks, but somehow I don't think you mean it."

"Oh, yes, I do. I am sincere in my congratulations, but…"

"Of course. There is always a but," Thom says as he smirks while rolling his eyes.

He is physically and emotionally exhausted and is in no mood to play this game. If she were any common prowler, he would have had thrown her in prison without saying another word. Yet, for some reason, he wants to hear what she has to say.

"I have been waiting for this moment for 19 years," she replies with a smile.

Nineteen? That's Thom's age. His heart starts to pound. In the back of his mind, he knows exactly what she is trying to say, but he is afraid to admit it. No, he is too scared to even *think* it. Not daring to hear the next thing she has to say, he looks away, as if that is going to make it any more bearable.

After a moment of silence, Lenore continues, "I work at the Sovereign's office. I have been for a long time, well before Garret took over the position."

"That doesn't sound so bad," Thom says to himself.

It's definitely *not* what he thought she was going to say to him, but that's fine by him. A part of him thinks that she is starting off slowly to make it easier on him, but he knows very well that there is something important left to be said and he is afraid to bring it up.

"I have worked there for one reason and one reason only," Lenore says.

It's a teaser sentence if Thom has ever heard one. Even though his head is shouting, "What is that reason?" he keeps his mouth shut to hear her say it.

"Working in that office, I get to hear about everything that goes on in Balavan, everyone from children in schools to new recruits with the Desiderios, as well as spies from Trozos."

Puzzled, he is not sure what to think of the statement. On one hand, everything she has mentioned is related to him some time during his life. On the other hand, she may just be listing these things to pique his interest so he will continue to listen to her. Perhaps, she is not going to say what he *thinks* she is going to say after all.

"What are you saying? That you are a spy?" Thom interrupts.

Smiling, she says, "You can say that, but that is not what I am here to say."

"Please get to it, then," Thom says impatiently as he unintentionally holds his breath.

Taking a deep breath, she finally addresses the elephant in the room: "I am your mother."

Staring at her blankly, Thom steps back just a little bit. Then, he finds himself studying her face to look for resemblances, much the same way he did Fouke's severed head, but he doesn't see much. Instead, she looks like

235

someone else he knows – Amelia. She has straight blond hair and piercing blue eyes, just like Amelia. Now, it makes sense why the Richardsons chose her baby. That also explains why she looks so familiar.

"You look just like your father, may god rest his soul," Lenore says as she looks at the ground as a tear comes out of her eyes.

"Who is, or *was*, he?" Thom asks as he closes his eyes, knowing full well what the answer is, but he has to hear it from her.

"Major Brandon Fouke," she whispers with a quiver in her voice.

Then, a long silence ensues as he stares blankly again. After what seems to be the longest minute in the world, he puts his gun down on the night stand and sits down on his bed. Despite what he has suspected, it's very different to hear it out loud.

"You are exactly what he has hoped for – so brave and handsome. He would have been very proud of you," Lenore finally says as she manages to keep from sobbing out loud. Tears run down her face anyways.

Those words are too much for him. As he turns to face the wall, tears flow down his face for the first time since he got out of diapers.

"Snap out of it!" Thom chastises himself.

He should be joyful that he has found his birth mother, not that he has been searching for long since he didn't know that she was missing in the first place. All of this time, he has thought Amelia was her. Now that he knows the truth, the mother he has always known seems like a distant memory. It's odd really. It's almost as if the woman he has grown to love and respect has turned into a virtual stranger in that split moment.

He is not even sure if he knows her at all. Who is Mrs. Richardson really? Yes, she has done her best to be a mother to him, but it was all a lie. He has always wondered why she always keeps a slight distance from him. He has always discounted those chilling moments to her need to keep up her persona as the Generalissimo's wife.

Then again, he does remember how she tried to be caring. Even though there were even days when he thought she had to force herself to show affection towards him, at least she made an effort. Despite their estranged relationship, they did have some great times together, especially when he was younger. He cannot ever forget that. Genetics or not, she *is* his mother.

He just now has another one. While this sounds a little weird, it is his new reality. After failing to bond with Fouke before it was too late, he is not about to make the same mistake with Lenore. This is the opportunity he has been waiting for. He cannot let another moment go to waste. There is no telling if someone, like Mrs. Richardson, may barge in any minute to take her away.

After composing himself, he clears his throat and says, "It's a pleasure to finally meet you, Mother."

Upon hearing him call her that, Lenore breaks into a wide smile, the same one Thom has when he has a good laugh with Max. She runs towards him and gives him a big hug.

"I have so many questions. I don't know where to start," Thom confesses.

"I take it you read my journal entries," Lenore says.

After seeing Thom nod, she says, "You probably want to know how they got in your pocket."

Nodding again, Thom admits he has been quite curious.

"My dear friend Torgny put it there."

"What?" Thom says in disbelief.

"Why do you think he sent both you and Russell to Trozos?"

"I honestly don't know. I only know Violet's version, but I have always thought that was just a cover story."

"You are right. Torgny and I have been friends and confidants for a very long time. After I told your father about you, he abandoned me. I couldn't tell my parents. I also couldn't count on any of my friends from high school. They wouldn't understand. Torgny was there when I needed a shoulder to cry on. Ever since then, I have always been able to count on him," Lenore replies.

"Are you in love with him?"

"Oh, goodness, no! He is old enough to be my father!"

"Sorry. I have to ask. From my experience, men don't usually bend backwards for a woman unless they are in love or want something from them."

Even though he doesn't usually get into other people's personal business, this is different. Her business has just become his business.

"Well, he may have feelings for me, but I have made it perfectly clear that our relationship is purely platonic. After so many years, I would think that we have an understanding."

"So, that explains why he was following Amelia. He didn't do it for his chief. He did it for you."

"Yes, I want to know everything there is to know about the woman who is playing my role in my boy's life."

"Why did you tell him to send Russell there?" Thom asks, trying to understand her logic.

"I know it's a mistake, but I couldn't bear not seeing him any longer. I was hoping that by sending inexperienced

238

boys like Russell there, he would be able to come back unharmed."

"Why didn't you wait before sending the Desiderios after him?"

"I got impatient. I knew they would send you and you would be able to find him faster than anyone else would. You have always been very good at your job. Ironically, you were *too* good at it. Now, I know I was wrong. I underestimated you. Never in my wildest dreams did I think that it would end with your father's death," Lenore says as she looks at the ground as her voice shakes again.

The guilt has returned to Thom in full force.

After a moment of silence, Thom sheepishly says, "I cannot tell you how sorry I am."

"No, I am the one who should be sorry. The fault is actually mine, not yours. If only I hadn't been so careless, none of this would have happened. You were only following orders. Besides, you didn't know the real him. You thought you were capturing a murderer who contributed to the destruction of the dominion for the last six years. Who can blame you?"

"You still love him, don't you?"

Nodding, Lenore admits that she has never stopped loving Fouke despite knowing what kind of man he really is.

"In my heart, I know he always loved me, too. Even though he acts like he wants nothing to do with me or you, he has made many effort to be close to us. For one thing, he always came into the sovereign's office to ask me insignificant questions at least once a week. It's as if he just wants to check up on me without letting anyone else know that we share a past. For another, he hated the military. He never wanted to be a part of the Legionnaires. He only joined because he knew being closer to Victor would mean being closer to you. It tore him apart. Eventually, it also made his heart black."

Thom is dumbfounded by what she said.

"So, what you are saying is that all of this time when he acted like he couldn't stand me, it was all an act?"

"Yes, if he didn't, he was afraid that he would reveal his true identity to you. The Richardsons have made us swear to never do that, but after losing Brandon in such a tragic way, I cannot waste another moment with you. With Victor dead, I don't think Amelia can do anything to me now. Even if she tries, I have nothing left to lose anymore besides you."

Those words warm his heart. Without uttering the word, Lenore has shown that both she and Fouke have always loved him and have watched him grow up to the man he is today. Despite his own misgivings, a part of him is glad that they did. At least now he knows why Fouke had nothing to say at the end of his life and why he changed into a person he almost didn't recognize. It wasn't simply because he was too ashamed to have been caught for the heinous crimes that he had committed or the fact that he had nowhere to go. It was because the sight of his own son made him realize how far off the deep end he'd gone and that there was no turning back.

Epilogue

With Thom and Russell's teams gone, Chief Cai can finally rebuild his village. It was a hard lesson to learn. He can no longer hide in his own shell or the mask of a cannibalistic tribe, living in denial and pretending that the rest of the world has stopped revolving just because his tribe has. He will have to modernize if he intends on protecting his people.

He vows he will never make that mistake again. Without an escaped war criminal on the run, there is no reason for anyone from Balavan to go search in deserted islands, but that does not mean that someone else from another country will not. He just has to be ready when, not if, the next time it happens again.

The only consolation is he knows that he still has good people like Nonni and Grami who maintained their vigilance. If it were not for them, there is no telling what Fouke would have done. Despite their appearances, they were highly trained intelligence officers in their prime. In fact, they were trained with Torgny and even went on the same missions together. Unlike Torgny, however, they have chosen not to leave the island because they could not bear to be away from their friends and loved ones.

In hind sight, that could be the reason why Torgny has no problem being away from home for such an extended period of time. With no real family left, he chose to make Balavan his new home, which led to the disastrous attack on the island. Although neither he nor Lenore meant for any harm to come to the villagers, it happened anyways.

For his decades of loyal service, however, Chief Cai decided not to punish him, but has chosen to exile him from the island forever. Although he had not been back to Trozos for many years, Torgny misses it now that he is no longer allowed to be there. He will just have to live with the knowledge that he has led to so much pain and suffering back home.

At least, Violet can now rest easy. Without Fouke, the dreams of the La Rivincita are crushed. They have all held their hopes and dreams of a revival on the only man who escaped El Diablo and the Warrior, which somehow gave him a legendary status almost equal to theirs. Now that they know that he was merely a human, who died like a common criminal, they no longer have the energy to continue their fight. Following Russell and Iris's advice, the La Rivincita has all but disbanded.

After his triumphant return, Thom has been promoted again, this time to the rank of Brigadier General. As his previous promotion, he feels no joy in it, but to other members of the Desiderios, he seems to be happier now, but not for the reason they think. On the surface, he seems to have come to terms with his guilt, but the truth is he will never be able to get over it.

How can anyone be able to forgive himself for being personally responsible for the demise of not one, but two, of his fathers? The only solace he has is the knowledge that he now has his birth mother by his side. He knows that one day; he will find a way to truly redeem himself. For now, he can only live one day at a time.

About the Author

Megan H. Lee is a college student in North Carolina. She started writing books in elementary school and has kept her passion for literature. The idea of the Balavan series started when she was in middle school, and years in the making have contributed to make the book. This is her second novel written in collaboration with her mother Sylvia S. Lee, who adds to the intrigue and suspense of the series with her love of history and imagination.